Penguin Crime Fiction
Editor : Julian Symons
Deadhand

George Sims was born in London in 1923, and was
educated at the Lower School of John Lyon, Harrow. He
served for five years in a Special Communications Unit in
the Army, and then became a dealer in rare
manuscripts. He enjoys travelli
Mediterranean an
his hobby of
cars and is al
novels, *The T*
Last Best Frie
available in Pe
have three child

Penguin Books Ltd, Harmondsworth,
Middlesex, England
Penguin Books Australia Ltd, Ringwood,
Victoria, Australia
Penguin Books Canada Ltd,
41 Steelcase Road West, Markham, Ontario, Canada

First published by Victor Gollancz 1971
Published in Penguin Books 1974

Copyright © George Sims, 1971

Made and printed in Great Britain by
Hunt Barnard Printing Ltd, Aylesbury, Bucks
Set in Linotype Plantin

The Human Situation from which there is a brief quotation on page 103 is by Macneile Dixon, published by Edward Arnold

This book is sold subject to the condition that it shall not, by way of trade or otherwise, be lent, re-sold, hired out, or otherwise circulated without the publisher's prior consent in any form of binding or cover other than that in which it is published and without a similar condition including this condition being imposed on the subsequent purchaser

George Sims

Deadhand

Penguin Books

How easy for Neville the transition from libertine to prig! Effortlessly he slid into the second role – it was made for him. Sydney Mansell – he mentally admonished – you allow your wife too much liberty! With an Othello's gaze he could visualize Gerald reaching out to touch those nacreous thighs and tracing the line where the sun-tan ended. Then, much worse, the picturing of Rachel undoing the buttons on Gerald's shirt and tugging impatiently at his belt.

She treats me badly at times, he thought, then shook his head wonderingly as a more detached part of his mind intervened to point out that his complaint was a subject fit only for a maudlin song. Unfaithful! How absurd it was to brood like this. It was all right of course for him to be unfaithful to his wife and to cuckold Sydney Mansell, but everyone else must toe the line.

'Mm – yes – bits and pieces,' Rachel said reflectively, gazing intently into the wall mirror as she painted a line across an eye-lid.

'What?'

'Just that, darling. It reminded me. Sydney asked me the other day if you were still dealing in "bits and pieces".'

'Cheek!' Neville hovered for a moment on the edge of being uncomplimentary about Sydney Mansell, though he knew it was a primary rule for an adulterer not to criticize the husband.

'Not really. Just his way of putting things. I liked it. I was able to praise you, darling. Said you were thriving. Said you had wonderful taste . . .'

Sydney Mansell was a thrusting, restless, endlessly ambitious tycoon in the textile world with several showrooms and warehouses in the Mortimer Street 'rag trade' area and an impressive block of offices in Bruton Street. Employing several hundred people, owning a booming business considered ripe for a takeover by the industrial giants, it was not surprising that in his eyes the activities of an antique dealer with a small shop tucked away in St Christopher's Place and one aged spinster assistant appeared piffling.

'Anyway, the point is I have this birthday coming up and

he said would I like to choose something at your shop and I said yes thank you very much. That's his idea of buying a present – to let someone else get it and preferably wholesale . . .'

She stopped talking for a while as she put on her bra, turning her back to him for it to be fastened. She said that she had begun the affair because she wanted the love she did not get from her husband. That was her excuse. What was his own? Was it all just a self-deluding, narcissistic fantasy?

'Never mind, it gives me a legitimate excuse for popping in quite often at St Christopher's Place. Now if you only had a cosy couch in that back room . . .'

'What about my Miss Patterson?'

'Don't worry, I shall not be shocking Alida Patterson. Just remember to put some nice things aside. With Sydney's cash and your expertise I'm bound to do very well. Button me!'

Neville sniffed as he stepped forward obediently to fasten her chiffon blouse. 'You smell delicious.'

'Just something from a bottle, darling. Anyone can buy it. Butterfly Orchid.'

But who had bought that particular bottle? She had probably forgotten telling him that she never bought perfume for herself. Had Sydney Mansell sent someone out to perform that little chore or was this more evidence of a rival – possibly Gerald? Picking up these vague hints gave Neville the faintest inkling of what it must be like to be blind and hear laughter in the dark and be forced to guess what was going on.

'One or two more of those honey-tasting kisses, then I must be off.' She slipped her arms inside his dressing-gown and clasped him round the waist. She had a blend of sexual aggression and submission for which he had always hankered, but there was more to his obsession with her than that: he wanted her physically but the sexual conquest was only a step towards a vital emotional end. When she surrendered to him, calling out his name again and again in her climax, she convulsively gave him something apart from her body, something he had to have.

After they had kissed she cuddled up against his chest,

content to stay still and quiet in his arms for a while. The Nancy Sinatra record still whirling in the living-room had reached the 'Let it be me' song, appropriate to their imminent parting.

> Each time we meet love
> I find complete love . . .
> If for each bit of gladness
> Someone must taste of sadness
> I'll bear the sorrow . . .
> Let it be me . . .

Neville was thinking that Mansell's random inquiry about him might have a significance that had eluded Rachel. He remembered his solitary, uninterrupted conversation with Mansell in which he had the uncomfortable feeling of being like a beginner at tennis knocking up with the professional. Mansell brought all his weighty and foresighted intelligence to bear on each problem that confronted him. No doubt Rachel was an expert in the pursuit of clandestine pleasure, but she was also inclined to be reckless and careless about their assignations. Perhaps Mansell had become aware of his wife's unfaithfulness and was now making the first, subtle steps to deal with it, like the preliminary skirmishing steps made by a chess master to obtain a foreseen end.

When the Nancy Sinatra song ended Rachel sighed a trifle theatrically and moved out of Neville's arms. He spied one of her hairpins under the hand-basin and automatically bent down to pick it up, meeting her amused gaze.

'And are we expecting a visit from the Inspector of Adultery then?' she inquired. 'Didn't you say Helen was in the south of Ireland and would be there for about two weeks?'

'Absolutely right.'

'Well surely you don't have to scurry about with your dust-pan and brush?'

He assumed a mock chastened look, nodding and saying 'Very true.'

'So poor Helen is having to cope with two children and a horse-drawn caravan?'

Poor Helen. That was the second time recently she had

used that adjective to describe Helen. Neville grimaced at her and said 'In self-defence I must point out that it isn't a matter of *coping* with anything. She likes horses and caravans and mooching along quiet lanes in County Cork, and so do the children. Anyway she's got her sister with her to help . . .' He imagined himself walking along listlessly, leading a horse, the personification of boredom, and knew he had been right, for his family's sake as well as his own, to plead pressure of business as an excuse for not going. Then he did a double take and gave Rachel a gentle push into the hall. 'Quite fantastic! You've got me nearly apologizing for existing, defending myself for staying here and yet it was you who said I *must* find some excuse so that we could slip away for a day or two in Suffolk.'

Rachel laughed. 'Quite true. You see – Sydney's right – I'm an absolute bitch! But I do want you to come to Suffolk. I'm off there tomorrow to my aunt's cottage . . .' She hesitated as she dealt with some problem in her mental timetable. Neville just managed to suppress a comment on her conveniently situated aunt. She seemed to have an army of relations and accommodating friends strategically placed throughout the country.

'Give me a day to settle in and to make sure the coast's clear. I'm going to have the cottage to myself while my aunt pops over to Brittany for a week or so, but I'll be easier in my mind when I've actually seen her depart. Phone me without fail at Walberswick the day after tomorrow then . . .' She reached forward to hold his arm and squeeze it. 'Then, my paramour, make tracks for Suffolk, as fast as that crazy Alfa Romeo will take you. A whole night in your arms, *quelle luxe.* Or, better still, make it two nights. I think you'd find more than forty-eight hours would become a bit claustrophobic. Just the sea and the marshes and me . . .'

'Sydney won't be going there then?'

'Sydney doesn't care for the sea or the marshes. And he can have me any old time without driving a hundred miles for it.' The second sentence came out in a slightly bitter, taunting tone, as if that was a situation he should deal with. He said nothing but looked deep into her blue eyes, trying to discover what she really felt. Their relationship had nowhere to go: Rachel was usually the one who faced this squarely while he deluded himself with a farrago of romantic dreams and desires, but occasionally she would make an enigmatic comment that might be intended to change the nature of their liaison.

With a flourish she produced an envelope from her handbag and waved it in front of his eyes as if to dissipate what she had just said. 'Here you are. Phone number and complete directions plus one small sketch-map. You'll see my aunt's cottage is in the Squireshill Marshes at Walberswick. Next to the Tinker's Marshes, my devil, my tinker! But I want you to drive to Southwold and park there. Southwold and Walberswick practically face each other across the mouth of the river Blyth. Walberswick is a tiny place and if that flashy pillar-box-coloured car of yours spends a night with my mini it might attract comment. Masses of anonymous parking space in Southwold, however, so proceed from there to walk over the common and cross the Bailey bridge to Squireshill Marshes. You'll like that secret approach! Very romantic, particularly by moonlight! The sea-wind in the reeds, gulls flying overhead. Perhaps I'll put a lamp in the window . . .'

He moved his head from side to side in silent amusement at the explicitness of her instructions. It was always like this when they met out of London. He was given foolproof directions and would not have been surprised to be issued with a packed lunch. But once they had been delivered Rachel moved along the passage to the stairs which led down to the front door, and Neville thought of how empty and lifeless the flat would seem when she had left: and he welcomed the Daniel Priest 'treasure-hunt' that would take him out of it for the rest of the evening.

At the top of the stairs he reached out for her suddenly, pulling her off balance. Her belly was pressed against his thighs and his blood stirred. He bent down to kiss her neck, moving his knee against her thigh and just brushing her nipples with the backs of his fingers, and she shuddered with sensuous excitement, throwing back her head in an ecstasy of abandon. At moments like this her scented body became a drug. How well he understood all the madness, obscenity and jealousy of desire.

She took a step down to regard him with a cool, judging look as if to estimate whether it would be worth her while to return to the bedroom, then shook her head: 'Yes, it's an ardent temperament. Don't worry darling, I'll give you a marvellous reference when we part.'

Holding her head in his hands he wished he was unpinning the strands of black hair so thick and springy that it felt as if her skull was padded, and it was time for their lovers' games to begin, not end. Foolishly he asked. 'Do you love me?'

'Yes. Of course,' She spoke in an impatient, clipped way like a Noël Coward heroine to convey that she found this question irritating. She flashed a glance at her minute watch. 'Don't lose that wonderful hairy chest!' She added this in a tone of bantering inconsequence, idly flapping the lapel of his dressing-gown. He could never think of suitable replies to her teasing remarks and later the silliest of them would return to him, taking on another significance.

'Yes, folks . . . ' She paused as she felt behind her for the lever to open the front door. 'Mr Softy is alive and well and living at Montagu Mews West.'

She was right of course. '*Lacrimans exclusus amator*', the tag about snivelling lovers, was one of the very few quotations he remembered from Latin lessons at school; a prophetic act of retention.

'Now, how's your memory? What is that number you must phone without fail the day after tomorrow?'

'Candlestick 999.'

She shook her fist at him and disappeared out of the door.

2

Torschlusspanik. Some German psychologist had come up with the apt phrase, 'the panic of closing doors', to describe that period in a man's life, perhaps late thirties or early forties, when the doors of life begin to close and he loses the sense of all things being possible. Environment, family, career, income – all tend to become fixed, and the man begins to run out of options. One of Neville's contemporaries had defined middle-age as being the period of 'an alertness for grievances, a sense of lost opportunities, frustration and an old-maidish absorption in the small print on patent medicine bottles'. It was in moments like those that followed close on Rachel's departure that Neville could see himself clearly as a typical victim of *Torschlusspanik*, trying the classic cure of a younger woman, and did not like what was under the microscope.

When he returned to the living-room the Nancy Sinatra record had finished and Nat King Cole was singing, ironically, 'Just you, just me', then the record-player clicked off and the flat became silent. A single fly endlessly circled the central light fixture, underlying his feeling of profound loneliness.

The tray of tea things stood by the couch and the empty Asti Gancia bottle lay near it; his shirt peeled off by Rachel's expert hands had been flung behind a chair; his socks and shoes made a trail leading out to the bedroom. As Neville began to clear the debris his mood of self-criticism intensified. His wife Helen was forty-five too but she did not complain about 'closing doors' or spend her life relentlessly pursuing some futile means of escape: she had inner resources which enabled her to be more mature, to accept things as they came, letting her youth and the past fall behind her. No doubt that Sydney Mansell at fifty-two was like that also, having a positive approach to life, ambitious and energetic, always planning for an expanding future.

Neville put the cups and glasses in the kitchen sink and went into the bathroom to wash. The man in the mirror looked liverish and the scar on his neck and shoulder was as red as if someone had just rubbed it. 'How perverse of you . . . ' – the phrase of reproach to Rachel because she had suggested he would find more than two days of her company claustrophobic came unsummoned into his mind, as if someone else had spoken the words: during the next few hours he could expect other similar visitations, eloquent replies and snappy wisecracks, a few subtle, probing questions he should have put to her. There was no doubt she always wanted things her own way; it was typical that she should try to find out so much about him, from touching his teeth to see how many gaps there were at the back to intimate details about Helen, but his own questions were skilfully eluded. I'm a fool, he thought, but I'm all I've got. That was the essence of the problem. One had to work with basic qualities shaped by heredity, background and upbringing, and it was difficult to change these.

While straightening the bedclothes he smelt the verbena scent again. This time he realized it was connected with the memory of a specific garden, one he could nearly visualize, hovering just beyond the edge of the bright screen on which he scrutinized people and places, stubbornly refusing to reveal itself. He knew that the memory was tied up with that of another scent, the unique and rather strange one of blackcurrants – in an overgrown garden where the bushes had run wild, forming a veritable wall with tall weeds and nettles . . . The counter of memory bowled along as if it would never come to rest, then wobbled uncertainly and fell into place.

Verbena – the funny sad memory was of a sweltering hot July day that he had lived through in the Inde et Loire area of France in 1944. Another week would see the twenty-sixth anniversary of that particular day which had been immediately followed by twenty-four hours that would always remain vivid in his memory.

On the 13th of July 1944 he and two other wireless operators in the Phantom Signals, CSM Duff Gordon and Sergeant 'Curly' Benbow, had been dropped by parachute near Vierzon on the river Cher. Their job had been to contact a Jedburgh team, a uniformed party operating in that area co-ordinating the local *maquis*, and provide communications for them.

The drop, which also involved two B mark II transceivers, each weighing thirty pounds and packed in suitcases two feet long, had gone off without a hitch, the only casualty being one of the removable crystals. They had fallen within a hundred feet of each other and the reception committee of *maquisards*, but had been informed that the Jedburgh group were in hiding near the ancient cathedral town of Bourges, having been forced to cover by the activities of an SS division making an intensive drive against *l'armée secret*.

For a week the three of them had been hidden away in a bombed, derelict cottage on the outskirts of Vierzon, just waiting for their contact. They had made a good team: both he and Benbow were better than average operators, and Benbow was also a good technician with the top instrument mechanic's rating, while their leader Duff Gordon was a man entirely without nerves who turned dicey situations into jokes. When they had been scooping up their parachutes after their first training drop at Ringway, Gordon had said to Benbow, 'Why aren't you in a fucking tree then?', exorcising the story of the agent Count Dzieŕgowski which had worried most people during training. Benbow in particular had taken the story of the gallant Count, who had dropped into a tree and was so badly hurt that he spent three days in hospital before continuing with his mission, very much to heart, and had often lugubriously estimated their own chances of doing the same thing.

Neville's strongest memories of the days spent cooped up in the rat-frequented hovel in Vierzon were to do with Gordon's ice-cool character. To hear him joking about their chances of survival, to see him going to sleep on a pile of filthy curtains as if he were dozing off in the Sergeant's Mess at Whaddon, had been salutary. Neville's own training had been enlivened by a number of anecdotes about Duff Gordon at Dieppe, where he had been one of a handful of British soldiers taking part in the aborted Canadian raid, and on a clandestine mission in Yugoslavia; but to actually experience his behaviour when they were surrounded by an SS division was something quite different. And eventually Gordon had given Neville the strongest possible proof that he did not waver when life and death were in the balance.

The comic memory associated with verbena was of the afternoon when he and Gordon had come downstairs, after some time spent in deciding how best to string out their seventy-foot aerial, to discover that Benbow was missing. For a moment Neville had felt apprehensive, but when he had questioned Gordon with a glance the reaction was typically matter of fact and to the point. Gordon had simply said 'Gone for a Jimmy Riddle' and then walked out to verify this; Neville had joined him in pushing through the blackcurrant bushes and lemon verbena to come upon Benbow peeing and singing very quietly 'Dearly Beloved'. Noticing his audience had not discomposed Benbow at all and he had concluded the ludicrous performance by shaking off the last drops as he sang:

How clearly I see
Somewhere in Heaven
You were fashioned for me . . .

Snapshots of Benbow: the sloppy soldier challenged by M.P.s in Bedford for having his battle-dress unbuttoned and found guilty on four other charges of slovenly behaviour, including that of carrying sandwiches in his gas-mask pack. G. H. Benbow the professional wireless operator, taking the fastest sending that a naval 'sparks' could manage, then acknowledging with QRQ 'send faster'. Benbow the devotee of ballroom dancing, unconscious of being observed, practising the rigid turns, exaggerated long steps and swooping dipping movements. Benbow saying 'dah dit dah dah dit', ‘end of message’, to stop some barrack-room lawyer’s speech. It was strange to think that Benbow would always remain aged twenty-three for Neville – as a child who dies young stays one forever.

The sad part of the memory was its association with the events of the following day when he and Benbow had been busy in the tiny parlour, checking over the wireless-sets while Gordon was still asleep upstairs. Benbow had been complaining about the likely inadequacy of their signal: the frequency range on the B mark II transceivers was wide enough, from 3.5 to 16 megacycles a second, but the signal was weak because the set could not produce more than 20 watts. A pessimist by nature, Benbow was notorious for his frequent use of Q S B ‘are my signals fading?’ when using one of these suitcase sets. His long face, surmounted by black hair as glossy and curly as the young Charlie Chaplin’s, was suitably glum as he made dismal predictions. Suddenly the door had been shouldered open to reveal a massively built S S *Scharführer* who had killed Benbow with a shot in the chest and then used his rifle like an axe to knock Neville to the floor. The pain had been intense but Neville had not lost consciousness, staring up and waiting for another blow to finish him off. Instead the German lieutenant’s face had crumpled and contorted as blood jetted out from his stomach. Duff Gordon stood on the stairway firing a second burst from his sten-gun which made the German’s body jerk about in a convulsive fashion. Then Gordon, his face showing no emotion, had stepped carefully across the shambles that had been contrived in a minute to pick up the German’s rifle and exclaim: ‘Christ, you’re the lucky one young Ralph! It jammed.’

The ringing of his telephone summoned Ralph Neville back from his ghostly events of 1944. He went into the living-room to pick it up, and heard Rachel’s rather excited voice asking a question he found most curious: ‘Darling, you are quite sure you want to come to Southwold? I mean I realize now that I rattled on and on with all those instructions not giving you a chance to say anything. Will you be able to get away easily in a day or two? If not . . . ’ She broke off with a stifled exclamation that made Neville think someone had touched her: she was very ticklish and reacted strongly to sudden movements. He remembered only too well another phone-call she had made – to Sydney – while he was caressing her neck, suddenly dipping his hand down on to her breasts. Was it now the case of the biter bit? Was Gerald holding her or teasing her in some way? He remained silent for a moment, straining to pick up any noises in the background, then said: 'Of course I want to come. You know that. Any day, distance no object. I've never pretended to be indifferent. Perhaps that's a mistake – but I tell you the truth. I want you. The day after tomorrow if it can't be sooner.'

'Fine, darling. Well – until Southwold then. Good-bye. Much love.' The line went dead but Neville continued to hold the silent telephone for a moment, puzzled by the conversation. There was something decidedly half-hearted about her tone. Perhaps she had gone straight from him to a meeting with Gerald and the direct comparison had been completely in the younger man's favour. Rachel was thirty, and once when she had mentioned Gerald she had said 'Of course he's very young . . . ' It did look as if Rachel might be turning away from him, and he knew that when it came dismissal at her hands would be short and sharp.

A pile of unopened letters on the desk before him was mute testimony to the way he was neglecting his business in the rather ridiculous attempt to reach the ever-receding shores of romantic love. His assistant Alida Patterson had handed them to him after lunch when he had looked in at his shop briefly, his mind full of the imminent meeting with Rachel. Miss Patterson had said of the post 'A promising lot', and a few years before he would have been tearing them open enthusiastically. There were several from America including one from a Boston museum which would contain a sizeable cheque, one from a good customer in Versailles, a registered envelope from Barclays Bank. He picked up the registered letter as if weighing it in his hand, then replaced it with the others.

As he went back into the bedroom to finish dressing,

Neville was trying to foresee what his life would be like without Rachel: from childhood he had become used to attempting to mitigate unpleasant events by living through them in his imagination.

It was nearly two years since he had ascended a staircase close behind Rachel, knowing her only slightly, at a smart party where he had felt lost and bored. She had stood out from the other women, the trendy dressers, the would-be *femmes fatales* and the numerous haughty model types with sucked-in cheeks, jutting hip-bones and *noli me tangere* expressions. She was simply dressed, but the rather plain frock drew attention to her thin arms and frail waist contrasting with the opulence of her bosom. She had a slumbrous, indolent look as if she was waiting for someone to wake her up. Her proximity, the delightful tendrils of black hair against a white neck, the drinks that had made him mildly amorous, the merry expression in her eyes when they had caught his earlier in the evening – all these things had conspired to make him touch her lightly on the neck. She had swung round at once to confront him. 'Now exactly what does that mean?'

In the event it had meant many hours of happiness, a renewal of enthusiasm for places and events shared with her, some moments spent waiting for her to arrive when he was as nervous as a love-sick youth, and a pervasive sense of guilt, partly because he was cuckolding Sydney Mansell but mainly because he knew that, like the compulsive gambler, he was risking the only thing he did not really dare lose, his family's happiness. Helen trusted him and so did not question the absurd slips he sometimes made about places, times and people he was supposed to have been with, but he was continually aware that if she did find out about the affair it would probably end their marriage.

Neville wrested his mind away from the convoluted problem he found insoluble to the trivial one of what jacket he should wear for the Daniel Priest 'quaint party or treasure-hunt or whatever'. He had already put on dark blue trousers, a white shirt and a dark blue knitted silk tie. Daniel Priest had stressed the informality of the gathering and suggested wearing old clothes because the treasure-hunt 'may take you into strange places'. It seemed to be the right evening for the 't'eatrical' jacket that he had never worn. It was of dark grey cloth with a silver stripe that he had bought on an impulse in Ireland. He had thought it would make a pleasant, sober sports-coat, but his tailor Sol Meyer had made it up with disclaiming gestures. Asked to comment at the final fitting, Meyer had given a surprising verdict: 'So it's quite nice but a little t'eatrical'. Neville did not relish looking 'a little t'eatrical' but he had the feeling it was a matter of wearing it now or never. He put it on, gave his shoes a sketchy polish with a duster, then left the flat, realizing that he had not eaten all day, was pleasurably hungry and had time for a quick meal before he met Mr and Mrs Daniel Priest.

3

Mr Softy. Alive and reasonably well, he slammed the front door with the illusion of escaping from the trap he had so carefully contrived for himself. No doubt all the problems would be there when the door opened again but at least he could forget them for a while in the affable and urbane company of Daniel and Mary Priest.

Turning out of Montagu Mews Neville looked at his watch to see that it was 8.15 – he had only three-quarters of an hour before he was due at the Buccaneer and the taxi-ride to Berkeley Street would take up to ten minutes. The possibilities for a meal were narrowed to a quick snack in the Raw Deal or Anna's Kitchen. He hesitated, then remembered a spotless looking fish and chip bar he had noticed in Baker Street. He licked his lips and quickened his step. He never felt like eating before a rendezvous with Rachel, but afterwards his hunger was sharp and would provide the best sauce for the simplest food. A piece of fried haddock, some chips, and he would be as well fed as the Priests no matter how much they were spending on their gourmet's repast.

Standing in a queue at the fish-bar counter, looking at the items chalked on a board reminded him again of Benbow. 'Wot, no peas!' or some similar complaint from Benbow always marked their entry into the fish and chip shop which they had frequented when they were stationed in the Shorncliffe Barracks at Folkestone in March 1944. That spring had been very cold and they spent all day in the open air with only two or three dry cheese sandwiches to eat.

Neville watched the technique of the man putting the fish in the fryer and remembered one particular evening when Benbow's notorious clumsiness had enlivened their meal.

Coming out of the fish shop Curly's attention had been concentrated on his newspaper packet, extracting chips smothered in vinegar and salt, complaining that the batter was not of the quality he was accustomed to in Wigan. Neville had been walking in front with Duff Gordon when they had heard the sound of a skirmish and turned to see Benbow scuffling with four Polish soldiers, his fish and chips scattered across the pavement. Gordon had promptly knocked one of the Poles to the ground and in seconds all three of them were involved in a mêlée with 'the wild men from Warsaw'.

As Neville made his way to a table he smiled to himself remembering the progress of that fight. Both he and Duff Gordon had been useful boxers, contenders for the Light Heavyweight title for Eastern Command, and Benbow was no man of straw in a tussle, but the three of them had met their match that evening. The Poles were all members of a Penal Battalion just returned from Italy, serving sentences for violent crimes like rape and assault. The scrimmage had been a long and bloody one in which he had been floored three times by a tall blond who was more proficient with his feet than his hands.

Even so one lot of punishment had not been enough for them; the next evening they had gone back for more, arming themselves with the assistance of Corporal Patsy Dugan, a former stevedore and professional wrestler, who had a twenty-inch neck and biceps to match. It had been a good gambit but the Poles had shown more foresight by simply doubling their numbers. When eight of them had appeared Gordon had grinned and whispered futile advice – 'Snap those jabs and keep your punches short' – as though Queensberry rules were going to apply.

Neville sighed. He certainly did not regret that it was twenty years since he had hit anyone in anger but he was frankly nostalgic about the period when he had been nineteen, had felt as fit as two years' hard army training could make him, owned no possessions and, above all, had the feeling that he was going to do something really worthwhile in the struggle against the Nazis.

Hailing a taxi on the corner of Crawford Street, Neville knew that he had diagnosed the disease from which he was suffering and the reason for his mental journey back to the war period: a feeling of futility that dogged him remorselessly. He was tired of dealing in 'bits and pieces', yet doubted whether he could make a change to anything he would find more satisfying. Dr Johnson's sage advice had been, 'Why, Sir, you should press yourself into the generality of mankind.' But how could he do this – was there a *kibbutz* that would welcome a forty-five-year-old antique dealer? And how did one sustain a feeling of satisfaction or achievement – could Sydney Mansell really believe that it mattered if he introduced a computer into his office or extended his range of 'Teen-age Modes'?

'Why me, Corp?' Benbow had originated this catch-phrase when they had been on basic training by complaining: 'Why me, Corp? I'm no shit-wallah' when ordered to clean out the latrines. This querulous response had been taken up with enthusiasm by the other recruits, to be uttered aloud or sotto-voce whenever there was anything difficult or dangerous to be undertaken. On one occasion, when they were doing parachute-training at Manchester's Ringway Airfield, Duff Gordon had even managed to look like Benbow as he uttered it before dropping through the hole in the floor of the Whitley. The whining note of complaint had amused Neville but also irritated him then because he had been an idealist, volunteering for the Army when he was seventeen, enthusiastic about training, convinced that every effort was worthwhile. How ironic it was to think that in 1944 he could hardly imagine surviving the war, regarding the possibility of a peace-time existence as an arcadian dream, only to find the reality dissatisfying; while Benbow, who would probably have made a good citizen, husband and father, had died.

As the taxi sped round Manchester Square Neville made a conscious effort to leave 1944 by speculating about other possible participants in the Priest 'treasure-hunt'. He had known Daniel Priest and his wife Mary, expatriate Americans who preferred to live in London, for six years, during which time their relationship had changed from a purely business one into a pleasant but not very intimate friendship which he did not think would ever become any closer. Neville was a little envious of Daniel Priest; not of his dark good looks or his wealth, but of his charm and his ability to find quickly a common factor with anyone – these were qualities Neville would have liked to possess. Once he had seen Daniel comfort an old man dying in hospital with tender raillery, and wanted that ability for himself. Priest was always amiable and tolerant, his manner never aggressive; 'Ah well, there it is' was his comment if anything went wrong.

Neville made a face, suddenly struck by the possibility that Mrs Abrams might well be one of the Priests' other guests. Ruby Abrams, a New York Jewess, had come from a very poor family in Flatbush, building up a group of beauty salons to the point where she owned a house in Sutton Place and a renowned flat in Gilbert Street. An equally rich husband remained in the background, never leaving New York, the target of occasional wisecracks. A keen wit, she could be either amusing or intimidating. In collecting antiques she showed so much shrewdness that it was like doing business with a top dealer, and Neville always found her conversation stimulating, but his admiration was often mixed with irritation. He much preferred to see her alone: in the company of other people she was inclined to regard a meeting as a trial of strength in which she could demonstrate her insight into his fallible character. These attacks were signalled by aggressive opening-gambits such as 'Now listen Rafe . . . ', 'Let me talk . . . ', 'Don't bother apologizing . . . '. She had the habit of interrupting people half-way through a sentence, cutting it off as of no consequence, which Neville found as rude as staring fixedly at a toupee. Occasionally they achieved a relationship better than a wary truce – she would then let him finish sentences and sometimes give a sympathetic grunt which meant that all was well. She had popped into his shop two days previously but had appeared uncharacteristically half-hearted, and left without making a purchase. He had good reason to remember her brief visit as it had come on top of a disconcerting telephone call from Rachel which had made him think that their projected Montagu Mews meeting might be cancelled.

The taxi stopped half-way along Berkeley Street and Neville got out in front of the Buccaneer. He had met the Priests there on a few occasions but had always been put off by its club-like atmosphere: he preferred a pub where all the customers were treated as equals by the landlord. In the Buccaneer a clique of hard-drinking regulars made a stranger feel that he was intruding on private grief.

The Buccaneer was more crowded than usual but Neville immediately picked out Mrs Abrams' rather strident voice in the hubbub exclaiming: 'He's got more bounce than a junkie's cheque-book!' She was seated at the bar, between the Priests and a tall blonde girl. Daniel Priest said something quietly in response and Mrs Abrams shook her head, saying 'You really believe that, don't you.' The next minute her all-the-way-round eyesight had picked up Neville and she turned, saying 'Rafe!' as if she was glad to see him, then negated this by making an introduction to the girl: 'There you are Susan, Mr Malcontent himself.'

Daniel Priest got off his stool to make a proper introduction with a charming smile that somehow managed to convey his opinion that the girl should make her own judgement on Neville: 'Miss Latymer, Ralph Neville. Ralph, Susan Latymer . . .'

Mrs Abrams broke in: 'Rafe, you have the disgruntled look of someone who's inherited a garage in Venice! Stand here.'

Susan Latymer smiled and said: 'You're being hard on him.'

Neville grinned: 'Not at all. I need to be kept on my toes.' He was thinking how Mrs Abrams sometimes reminded him of a gaudy macaw climbing on a curtain. He made the cowardly decision to damp down her powder with a compliment: 'That's a wonderful dress, Ruby.'

Mrs Abrams was pulled up short for a moment. She said brusquely: 'Rudi Gernreich makes *all* my dresses so he must take the praise or blame.' She turned to Susan Latymer: 'If you're puzzled how I behave now with Rafe you should understand how he acted then . . . The see-saw, you know, was a great invention.'

Neville took the large glass of whisky which had appeared for him with a grateful nod to Daniel Priest. Mrs Abrams went on: 'Yes, don't tell anyone, and tell anyone you do tell not to tell anyone too . . . but the word is that American custom is not wanted at the Neville establishment in St Christopher's Place. Suddenly yet dollars are out of fashion. Isn't that so Rafe?'

Neville was allergic to an excess of gesture in other people and tried to ration his own, but his hands shot out as he asked: 'What, where, when Ruby? What did I do?'

'Do? – why nothing. That's the whole point. When I came in the other day to have a little chat you were like a wraith. The man who never was! I wondered in fact if you had had a facsimile Rafe Neville made to deal with the more tedious clients. Another of your customers was complaining too . . . '

'Oh! Who's that?'

'Harvey Buchanan.'

Neville shook his head: 'Mr Harvey Buchanan thinks I'm a sinking ship.' He mentally congratulated himself on this subtle way of saying that Buchanan was a rat. He explained to Susan: 'I'm an antique dealer. Times are hard for us in that there's been an explosion in the number of dealers coinciding with the supply of good items drying up. Mr Buchanan . . . '

Daniel Priest broke in diplomatically: 'Susan knows exactly what you do, Ralph. She's very interested in antiques and likes your book.'

'Really?' Neville found it hard not to stare at Susan Latymer with an expression of incredulity. His book on antiques had been a fiasco. It contained several sketchy chapters of interest only to a tyro and a few much too specialized: he had winced a hundred times at its self-indulgent form. Even the format was a constant source of irritation; he had wanted a small book but the publishers had insisted on making it a quarto with a photographic board binding that was too flimsy for its size. Warped copies of it still occasionally stared out at him from bookshop windows – like bandy children whom no one wanted to adopt. It seemed an extraordinary bit of luck that the first really enthusiastic reader he met should be a delightful-looking blonde with long green eyes and a retroussé nose. She had feathery glinting eye-brows which appeared to have been hand-graded. Her top lip was thin and short in relation to the bottom one so that when she smiled one saw a lot of her side teeth.

Susan nodded. 'Yes. It's true, I'm quite a fan – I learnt a lot from that book. Particularly the chapter on clocks and watches with those super illustrations. That beautiful example of the John Harrison Timekeepers – wasn't it made for Captain Cook?'

'You're right.' Neville added pedantically: 'A duplicate of J.H. No. 4 was made by Larcum Kendall, and Cook used it on his second Antarctic trip in 1772.' She had read the book. He saw that her sherry glass was empty and asked if he could get her another. The Priests were deep in conversation with the proprietor of the pub. Neville held the *copita* up to attract the attention of the jolly-looking red-haired barmaid, aware that Susan Latymer had made some comment on Mrs Abrams' famous 140-carat diamond ring. Ruby waved her finger about for a moment as she said with a malicious grin: 'You know there's a curse goes with it . . . ?' She paused a moment to get maximum attention before delivering the punch-line: 'Yes – Mr Abrams.'

When Neville had passed the glass of sherry to Susan, Ruby Abrams took a thoughtful sip of gin then asked him: 'And how is Helen?' Before he could reply she explained to Susan: 'He has this lovely, charming wife he keeps locked up in Wootton Bassett . . . '

'Minterne Magna in fact' – Neville added the scholarly footnote, but Mrs Abrams continued imperturbably: 'Wootton Bassett, while he lives this footloose and fancy-free bachelor existence in London. You see he likes to have his cake, eat it, keep a bit for Sundays . . . '

Neville explained: 'My wife hates living in London and I prefer to be in the country when I'm not working, so we have a small house in Minterne and I use a tiny flat in London from Tuesdays to Fridays.'

Mrs Abrams made one of her ugly Habsburg lip grimaces and said accusingly: 'I glimpsed you at that St Denis party, leaving with the glamorous Mrs Mansell. Someone said how drunk you were.'

Neville sighed inwardly. He had known that it was a bad mistake to accompany Rachel to that party, and had done so reluctantly. Now this super-intelligent parrot would be continually making pointed comments on their fleeting appearance together.

Apparently it was mollify Ruby Abrams night. Mary Priest, possibly in an attempt to ward off the threatened Neville inquisition, paid her a compliment but Ruby cut it short, saying: 'No, really I feel awful. You know, like Tristan Bernard who hailed an empty hearse like a cab, saying, "Are you free? . . ." '

As they laughed Neville noticed for the first time that Susan Latymer's face was pale with fatigue or nerves. He wondered if she was finding the evening more of a trial than a pleasure. He was puzzled by something else about her appearance but could not think what it was. She wore a simply cut, very brief sea-green shantung frock. Her only jewellery was a large aquamarine engagement ring. Her layer-cut hair shone and bounced when she moved her head. Her skin was flawless and unlined. He estimated her age to be twenty-three or four. He had detected a slight lisp when she said yes.

Daniel Priest leaned towards them and said in a confiding tone: 'Now regarding this treasure-hunt, clue-hunt rather . . . ' Mrs Abrams hovered in alert speculation, nodding as she did when she had no intention of interrupting; she was usually on her best behaviour where Daniel Priest was directly concerned. 'Mary and I took part in a very good one a few weeks ago and enjoyed it so much we thought we'd *try* to organize another. The rest of the questers are clued in but just in case you don't know the set-up . . . Those who take part go off, in twos or threes, to follow a trail. The clue-hunt can be for a theme, a historical event, a fictional motif. The one we followed took us to a tenement in King Street, a deserted railway station, an alleyway decorated with old Russian posters, then a flat empty except for a table set with supper and with copies of the first number of the *Daily Worker* and the *Communist* prominently placed. It wasn't difficult to get on to the Communist theme, but the actual subject of the quest was the train that took Lenin back through Germany to Russia. First pair or trio to get back to base with the right solution wins a small prize. I hope you're interested,' he added dubiously.

Mrs Abrams looked thoughtful: 'Really and truly I wish I was sipping tea in a shady hat in a Zoffany landscape. I ask myself am I up to a "clue-hunt" and echo answers No!' She watched Priest's face as she said this and finished on a brighter note: 'No, I'm joking. It could be fun. And I do know my London pretty well . . .'

Neville said: 'I'll second that.' He was not flattering her this time. Ruby Abrams was an Anglophile who knew London better than many Cockneys, taking pride in such things as having her English account in the smallest bank she could find in the City – Neville knew that the only thing that could tempt her away from it would be the establishment of 'Peppercorn & Farthing of Old Cheapside'.

In outlining the projected programme for the evening Priest had looked slightly anxious in case it did not appeal to his listeners. Finishing his whisky, he shrugged: 'Who knows – this may turn out to be one memorable flop. All I can say is we enjoyed the Lenin trail – in fact I enjoyed it more than any game since I was tutored in Monopoly by a charming English lassie over here in '39 . . .'

Mary Priest raised her eyebrows to show that this was news to her. Tall, dark and slim, she could easily have passed as her husband's twin, and they seemed to get even more alike as time went by. They had the same unruffled good manners and diffident way of talking. She said: 'Do go on, Dan! What charming English lassie?'

Daniel Priest adopted a stagey English accent as if he was reading out the introduction over the credits of a bad film: 'I was on a juvenile, ill-fated European tour that ended with us scuttling back for Boston in the September. But in the August, ah me that August! we were in an hotel perched high on a cliff above Torquay. And when it rained this girl and her little brother and I would play Monopoly and look down on the silent progress of the waves. She was dressed like Deanna Durbin – do you remember that style – the Juliet cap, the bobby-socks, the loafer shoes?' He got up from his stool, pretending to brush away a tear. 'But I think I'll try to end on a happy note. Are we set?'

Neville could tell that, despite the jokey climax, Priest's mind was still taken up with the memory of that far-off holiday, and responded to him; it was unusual to be given a clue as to what emotions might be hidden behind that calm façade.

4

Susan Latymer. When they emerged from the smoky atmosphere of the bar she put her hand on Neville's arm. 'Tell me more about this Tuesday to Friday arrangement. What does your wife think of it?' She looked directly into his eyes, not in a flirtatious way but as if to gauge better the truth of what he told her. There was something in her manner that told him she was someone's girl; he did not need the sight of her engagement ring to know that.

Neville breathed in some relatively fresh air and said: 'Well. Of course it's a far from perfect arrangement. But while I want to work in London it seems to be the only answer. Later on I may take a shop in the country. That's how I started in the antique business. I met my wife while I was in hospital in 1944 – she was a nurse then and her father owned an antique shop in Salisbury. When I was demobilized in '46 I went to work for him. One day I'll probably go back into that area . . . ' He flashed her a look to see if he had given her too much information about himself but she was listening with a flattering concentration – she had the preternatural gravity of a precocious child.

Berkeley Street was surprisingly busy with both traffic and crowds of people making their way up from Piccadilly. The Priests were walking ahead with Mrs Abrams. Daniel Priest had not said exactly where they were going but had signalled that they would be turning off left in the Curzon Street direction.

Neville began to experience a sense of gathering enjoyment. Party games were not much to his taste usually but the clue-hunt as outlined by Daniel, and particularly one planned by him, might be interesting. It was a fine warm evening with a violet-tinged luminous sky above them; further to the west the orange ball of a sinking sun made the edges of tiny clouds take on the colour that one sees at the heart of a fire. He found Susan Latymer sympathetic and thought there was a chance they might become friends.

She held his arm very lightly and looked round into his face and she asked: 'Do you have any children?'

'Yes. A girl of fifteen and a boy of six . . .'

He wondered if she would be interested in hearing something about little Benjamin. He was parsimonious in telling anecdotes about children to childless women like Rachel and Mrs Abrams, rationing them as he knew they were of rather specialized interest. As he brooded on this they were making slow progress through a crowded thoroughfare called Lansdowne Row, until they realized there was some sort of commotion a few yards ahead. A tall scruffy youth, dressed in a German army jacket and steel helmet with Waffen SS insignia and HELL'S ANGELS in big white letters across his chest, was pushing Daniel Priest backwards, saying: 'Is this your actual Daniel then? And your Lionel and your Nigel, I suppose. You should fucking look where you're going, Daniel.'

Neville saw that Daniel Priest was looking round with a rather lost expression – he appeared to live in the pious hope that people would always behave rationally. Priest made some sort of apology to the young bully but it was cut short by another push. Neville shouldered his way through the jostling crowd, noting the different reactions to this loutish behaviour – sly amusement and some kind of strange pleasure on the part of strangers, Mary Priest's disdain and Ruby Abrams's fizzing annoyance. Neville's own response was a mixture of irony and rising anger. The last time he had been directly confronted by someone wearing that uniform it had been *Scharführer* Sepp Geisler, a giant of a man toughened by four years fighting from Greece to Russia. It was a bad joke now to be threatened by this pimply youth.

Neville came up by the side of Priest, looking intently at the 'Angel's' rig-out, noting the Prinz Eugen, General Seyffardt, and Hermann von Salza sleeve-stripes, the Italian red eagle SS badge and the *Rex Bewegnung* medal. He felt there was a chance that his ‘t’eatrical’ jacket might be christened in the dust of Lansdowne Row. He interposed himself between Priest and the youth, warding off the latter with his open right hand, saying: ‘Push off, sonny, and rev your motor-bike. It’ll make you feel better.’

‘Well fuck you Jack.’ The youth pushed back but it was a half-hearted movement, lacking conviction. Neville was struggling to control his temper; he had to be sure that if it did come to a fight he did not make the youth pay hard for wearing a loathsome uniform. It would be all too easy to remember the screams he associated with that murderer’s outfit, become submerged in a red mist of anger, and clobber the boy. He had to concentrate on the fact that the jacket was worn foolishly as a kind of fancy dress, something to attract attention. He leaned forward and said confidentially, so that only the boy could hear: ‘Slow up unless you mean it.’

The youth looked at Neville more keenly, as if he was seeing him in a different light, and moved off to the right, murmuring something about ‘piss arrogant’. When he had gone a few yards he called back: ‘All right, but I may see you again, Jack.’

The crowd, which had been quiet and still while this minor confrontation was taking place, began to move again and chatter broke out all round. Neville grinned at Daniel Priest and looked round for Susan. Mrs Abrams took his arm as she joined them, saying to Susan: ‘When you’ve said it all about Rafe he’s not limp-wristed.’

After she had moved off to join up with the Priests, Neville said quietly to Susan: ‘And Daniel’s not limp-wristed either. It’s just that I’ve had a rough and tumble background which equips one better for dealing with would-be trouble makers.’

Mrs Abrams looked back and called out: ‘Rafe! We’re agreed. You handled that with aplomb.’

Neville shook his head. ‘Such praise from so unlikely a source. If she’s not careful I shall break out into a chorus of “When you walk through a storm hold your head up high . . .”’

Susan giggled then asked: 'But what did you actually say to him? Those few magic words . . .'

Neville shrugged. 'When I was in the Army one lesson I learned the hard way was never to make a threat you don't intend to back up if necessary. So I just asked that boy if he really wanted trouble. Of course he might have said yes and then there would have been an unseemly scuffle. Ideally I should like to have dealt with it on a much lighter level. Used a joking approach, perhaps the Cowardly Lion's challenge: "Put 'em up. Put 'em *uuup*!" It was that SS jacket that put me off my stroke. Difficult for anyone of your generation to understand of course, but I've a strong personal reason as the last time I was that close to a SS uniform the wearer hit me with a rifle and broke my shoulder, collar-bone and three ribs. Would have killed me too if a friend hadn't stopped him dead . . . But I must stop there, I'm rattling on a bit.'

'Not true. Where did it happen?'

'In France. We were a wireless team supposed to be operating behind the lines, but in fact we didn't do anything except hide. The SS were making an intensive drive then against the *maquis*. Our particular place was just to the north of Oradour. Have you heard of Oradour? The SS *Das Reich* 2nd Panzer Division was held up in a place called Souillac, fighting the French resistance people, and one of the SS company commanders was killed in the village of Oradour-sur-Vayres, to the west of Limoges. So in retribution they butchered several hundred people. What is even more horrible, they did it at the wrong village. At Oradour-sur-*Glane*. So you see.'

'Yes, I do see.'

The Priests and Mrs Abrams had turned up Chesterfield Street. Above them the sky was shaded from palest primrose to the colour of permanganate-and-water. Stepping before them were grossly exaggerated shadows. Several pairs of high heels clicked and echoed on the pavement. Neville was struck afresh by the treacherous thinness of our dream-like life.

Near the junction with Charles Street Daniel Priest stopped the little convoy. 'The clue-hunt begins in a house just round the corner. It belongs to a dear old girl, Lady Villiers, who lives in remote Herefordshire and hardly ever visits London. Most of the time the house is closed up, but her son is giving a party there tonight so temporarily we're joining up with his crowd. I might add some music but the house itself is full of clues. It's possible, I suppose, that someone may solve the puzzle on the spot.' He pondered this for a moment. Usually as a host he was imperturbable but this evening seemed to have him slightly on edge.

'Now for your badges. Quite essential I assure you so please don't take them off.' Priest handed out circular cards with the word 'Quest' printed on one side in red letters. Neville turned his over and saw that underneath the pin arrangement there were some lines of verse:

> Motley I count the only wear
> That suits, in this mixed world the truly wise
> Who boldly smile upon despair
> And shake their bells in Grandam Grundy's eyes

Neville smiled to himself. It was typical of Priest that the card should be finally printed and have a salutary quotation so that one would be loath to throw it away, like the charmingly engraved Christmas cards he sent.

'One more thing,' Priest continued. 'Mary has taken pity on you three and insists that, as you have not played the game before, I give you an additional clue. So here it is. Porphyria.'

'Oh, not fair!' Ruby Abrams exclaimed in a particularly loud and strident voice, sounding just like Ethel Merman. 'I mean. That wraps it up kids! Auntie Ruby's home and dry. The clue hunt is all over. That's all I needed. *Porphyria*?'

'Okay,' Priest relented. 'But I'm being pressured here. Haemophilia.'

'That's better?' Ruby Abrams wailed to show that it wasn't. Intensively competitive if she embarked on anything, she would want to win.

'Well, I do have an advantage there,' Susan said to Ruby. 'Like Ralph's wife I started off on a nursing career. Haemophilia? Literally, a tendency to bleed. A condition in which the blood clots slowly. Patients suffering in this way are known as, excuse me, "bleeders".'

'Charades,' Ruby suggested. 'Can we play Charades? I'm crazy about Charades.'

Daniel Priest led them round to the left at the end of Chesterfield Street into the part of Charles Street which looked as if it was a cul-de-sac, ending at the Red Lion pub. It was a London backwater that Neville liked and he knew that in fact it was possible to continue round to Hay's Mews and Waterton Street. One house at the end of Charles Street was a blaze of lights, with the front door open and people queueing on the steps outside.

Neville asked Susan: 'And what stopped your nursing career?'

'Simple. A man. As Helen will tell you, men have a habit of putting paid to that particular ambition.'

They made a halting progress up the steps and Neville was parted from Susan by a large woman smelling of apples, dressed in Red Indian gear with a ribbon round her forehead and a roguish expression, who said to him: 'Well, here we are, packed tight as a box of bees.'

As they entered the house a girl with a welcoming smile held their arms momentarily and explained: 'It's a creeping and whispering party above the ground floor. We've strung up – things – at waist-height and everyone has to creep below them. If you bang into them or say anything out loud then you must put something in the charity bowls.'

Daniel Priest might be experiencing the tensions of the host anxious that his plans should work out right, but Neville was feeling continually more pleasantly carefree. After another drink or two anything that evolved would be more or less enjoyable.

The hallway was pure Victoriana. Neville's eye was taken by an enormous mirror surmounted by an elaborate gilt ormolu design, with a vaguely Empire motif, involving sepoys, river gods, two nymphs and a pair of classical figures representing Asia crowning Britannia. Standing nearby a tall, languid young man said to an equally remote looking girl: 'Of course I know him. We were at Harrow together. We left under the same cloud.'

The loud, insistent beat of pop music was replaced by a record Neville recognized, that of George Shearing playing 'When Sonny gets blue'. Neville mentally rehearsed the only Noël Coward line he knew – 'Extraordinary how potent cheap music is!' – in case he got involved in a conversation with the bored Harrovian, but it did not work out that way. Ruby Abrams materialized at his side, saying with a flash of her dark brown eyes: 'Suddenly, Rafe, you have this cat-who-ate-the-canary look. Meeting your only fan has gone to your head.'

'My fan! That's good. She's a nice girl with good manners. By chance she'd read my book and said so.'

'No.' Something had caught Ruby's attention and she turned away for a moment, presenting Neville with her Queen Nefertiti profile. He was struck again by her chameleon-like trick of changing her appearance. 'Seriously. It's more than that.' She added this mechanically before turning to present him with her full face and attention: 'Apparently Mary Priest only met her for the first time at a Private View two weeks ago. Somehow your name came up and Miss Susan Latymer said right out she'd like to meet you. A forward minx, that one.'

Neville felt someone's eyes on him across the hall and saw Susan Latymer was standing in a doorway regarding him intently, as if he were a conjurer and she was bent on knowing how he did a trick. Suddenly he realized what it was about her that had puzzled him earlier in the evening. Apart from being nervous, she gave the impression of someone playing a part.

'There! You see. Now she's beckoning you. The sly puss!'

'Beckoning *us*, Ruby. Listen! That music. Dan said he might add some music as a clue. This is too much of a change from pop and jazz to be accidental. Beethoven's rather out of place at a party like this.'

'Beethoven? What is it?' Ruby shook her head wearily. 'You know, I have the feeling this game is going to be about as easy as looking someone up in the Moscow phone-book and names aren't listed alphabetically there.'

'It's a Beethoven piano sonata but I don't know which one. Well, what have we got so far? Porphyria. Haemophilia. This Victorian décor. A Beethoven sonata.'

Ruby sighed. 'Well, good for you Rafe. Just wave bye-bye as you go to collect your prize.' Apparently handicapped by a lack of knowledge in this particular contest, she was going to have to use all her guile. For a moment she wore a vulnerable look as she did on rare occasions when seeming dazed by a change of tempo and mood. Neville knew that she was basically a friend of his, despite the verbal attacks he suffered, and regretted the peevish whim which had prompted him to hide a superb quarter repeater made by Justin Vulliamy when she had called in at his shop. He took hold of her arm to propel her through the group that barred their way. She whispered: 'You know me, Rafe. I'd sooner have five years of fun than thirty of dull. But think before you leap. Believe me, Miss Latymer has ha-ha eyes when she looks in your direction.'

'You know me, Ruby. That's flattering and I can't pretend to dislike the idea, but you're wrong. Susan Latymer not only wears an engagement ring, she has a notice that says "I'm friendly but that's all so forget it".'

Neville could see only a sprinkling of people wearing Quest badges and no one that he knew. Everyone seemed anxious to enter the room into which Susan had disappeared rather than tackle the first charity obstacle, a ribbon with bells strung low across the stairs. Through a high balustrade Neville spied a cat's pale green eyes and thought how strange this sudden flurry of human activity must seem to the animal accustomed to a closed-up house.

When Neville reached the doorway which Susan had vacated he came on an interior like that in a photograph he had of 'Mrs Langtry's London Residence'. The crowd-drawing attraction was a buffet set out on two tables. Neville's professional eye noted an elaborate ormolu clock which he suspected was made by Howell and James. There were some superb Octavius Hill photographs on the wall nearest to him:

the 'Lessons in the Open Air' that combined such a high degree of definition with mysterious depths of shadow, and 'Conversation Piece' in which Hill demonstrated that penetration which made him a first class portrait artist. Neville would have liked to congratulate Lady Villiers on her family's taste.

The music coming from another room had abruptly changed again, Beethoven being replaced by something Indian. A man standing close to Neville, with the look of a voluptuary, weary and cynical, said: 'I'm of the firm belief that the sitar has all the musical range and content of elastic bands stretched over a cigar-box.'

Neville nodded approvingly, waiting his chance to join Ruby who had wormed her way through to the table. He listened to the smart chatter going on around him:

'Of course I love him – he spent hundreds of drachmas on me!'

'Mummy made me a homosexual.'

'If I gave her the wool would she make me one too?'

'So there was this rapist with the most unlikely line in dialogue: "I love you I love you I love you . . ." '

'What I say is sex is too good to be free. There must be a catch.'

'The Wheel of Karma turns. You know, Buddhist theology, he who died a dung-beetle returns a king. And vice versa of course . . . '

' 'Allo, dahlink . . . ' A small woman launched off nervously into a Greta Garbo voice, but Neville took his chance to join Ruby and Susan at the buffet table and lost the rest of the sentence, listening instead to a fat man saying drunkenly, 'Curaçao,' over and over again and smiling as if it was a good joke.

Susan and Ruby were fast in animated conversation so Neville surveyed some bottles, helped himself to a glass of Château Grillet 1958, and then was struck by a pang of conscience, deciding to bang into the first charity 'thing' he encountered. Sipping the delicious wine he studied an 1890s photograph of ladies dressed in high fashion of the élite which time, with its infallibly ironic touch, had rendered at once absurd and dowdy. A window behind the buffet table was uncurtained and he could see the quivering filigree of a single reflected bough. He took a plate and heaped it high with plump black cherries, catching the amused gaze of the cynic who had animadverted on the sitar. 'I'm greedy for cherries,' he admitted.

The cynic said confidentially: 'And girls too I expect. Tell me, have you ever bedded twins?'

Neville just stopped himself from naïvely exclaiming 'Good Lord no!' He had the mind-boggling vision of a romp with Rachel-twins. He tried to dismiss the apparition and said tamely, 'As it happens, no.' He noticed that his neighbour was not wearing the Quest badge. 'Apropos of nothing do you happen to know what "Porphyria" means?'

'As it happens, yes.' The matter was pondered in silence.

Neville indicated his badge. 'I'm involved in this party game and one of the clues we've been given is "Porphyria", but we don't know what it means.'

'Simple. It's the relief of losing your no-claim bonus, or of finally touching bottom.'

'Thanks but no thanks.'

'No, seriously, it means teaching a parrot to say, "Sit ye down" or "Scuse fingers" or coarser phrases inimical to the parrot's owner.'

Neville regretted having involved himself with this joker. He poured some more wine and murmured, 'Just a thought.'

'Porphyria – some kind of royal disease I think, I mean one associated with Royalty, like haemophilia. You'll be simply fascinated to know it turns urine the colour of port wine.' The joker shook his head to show he was disappointed by Neville's lack of humour and turned away.

The crowd coming in for refreshments had thinned out and Neville saw that Susan and Ruby were leaving the room. He caught another mysterious fleeting glance from Susan, like a message in code. He said: 'I've found out the meaning of "Porphyria". A disease linked with Royalty. A word I never heard of till this evening.'

Ruby said sourly: 'Don't be so humble Rafe. You're not so great.'

Neville mischievously confided to Susan: 'Actually Ruby does have the clue-hunt all wrapped up. She thinks it's the train that took Lenin back to Russia.'

Ruby sniffed. 'I'll do the funnies.'

Mary Priest met them in the doorway. 'Up one floor please. The clues really start there.'

5

The Quest. Neville followed a small group of people, all of whom were younger and livelier than himself, up the stairs, dutifully knocking into the charity barrier and making a small contribution, and then along an inadequately lit passage. As he did so the notion flashed into his mind that it was just possible that he was the subject of a hoax where Susan Latymer was concerned. Perhaps the Priests had been amused by the idea of producing such an unlikely 'fan' for him – this would account for his strong feeling that she was acting a part. Twenty years of solid experience in dealing with people had developed a kind of mental radar system in him with regard to human behaviour. It was an unlikely joke for the Priests to play, but the story of her reading his lamentable book and being anxious to meet him was even less likely.

From upstairs the sounds of revelry on the ground floor became a subdued, impassioned murmur. Mary Priest was waiting in a small room furnished as a study. She held her elegant hands over the tops of two bowls which stood on a desk. She said, 'First a word of apology,' lowering her voice and looking about her. 'Dear friends, please don't be angry with us if this clue-hunt is not much of a success. It is our first attempt at such a thing, and frankly . . . ' She paused to see that no one else was coming into the room. 'Frankly I think it's much more difficult than Dan and I ever imagined. So bear with us over any disappointments. Now you have to pick a counter from a bowl and then match counters to find your partners before setting off. I must tell you though that there's one hell of a good clue right here in this room.'

Ruby Abrams promptly scurried to a wall cluttered with framed insignia and photographs. Neville was standing right by a bowl and Mary Priest urged him to take a counter, saying, 'No peeking, mind.'

Some odd quirk made him keep his eyes very slightly open as he leaned forward, and simple vanity prevented him from choosing counters labelled 'Soap' and 'Stanley Laurel'. His fingers closed round 'Orpheus' and he shut his eyes firmly, opening them again to show suitably acted puzzlement about the name he had taken.

'Trouble is,' Mary Priest said to him confidingly, 'Dan has chosen a pet theme for this blessed clue-hunt. And it's one that's hard just to hint at and yet not give away . . . What is the matter with me? I can't stop apologizing. We had a man round the other day to sell us a new television-set and he could not stop saying, "very sincerely". Now I can't stop making excuses for this evening . . . '

'Well, at least you can stop with me,' Neville assured her quickly. 'I'm interested all right. What do I do if I should happen on the answer?'

'Report back here. This room is HQ. Come back by 1 a.m. anyway, or earlier of course if you decide to give up. You know what a perfectionist Daniel is – he wanted to try and fit each hunt . . . There I go again.'

Neville noticed that Ruby Abrams with a rueful expression was holding the 'Oliver Hardy' counter. He walked over to the wall covered with photographs, most of which appeared to be of royal groups. Royalty was a subject that had never interested him, and he could only identify the Czar of Russia, Queen Victoria and Kaiser Wilhelm. He moved on to study a framed vellum document with a heavy seal, inscribed on the mount in cobweb writing: 'Appointment of Lord Edmond Villiers as Envoy Extraordinary and Minister Plenipotentiary with Great Seal'. A feeling of claustrophobia, such as he experienced in museums, began to rise up in him and he turned away from the rather pathetic relics of pomp and circumstance. Daniel Priest had entered the room, with a courteous but strained expression, like the host at a hectic party which had gone on too long.

Neville pretended to be studying a delicate drawing of

heads of wild garlic while he concentrated on what pet theme Priest might have chosen to illustrate in the clue-hunt. He knew of only one Daniel Priest obsession – for the work of Vermeer – and that could not possibly be connected with Queen Victoria or royal diseases. He smelt a faint, elusive scent and the word 'Snap' was breathed into his ear. He turned to see Susan Latymer smiling at him, looking much more relaxed and natural than she had been earlier in the evening, holding out her counter marked 'Eurydice'. 'See whom you've been lumbered with,' she said coyly.

'Lumbered? I should have said my luck could not be more in. Obviously we *must* win. So where is the prize?'

'Ralph! Now I know why you succeed in business. The plums simply fall into your hands,' said Mary Priest, coming over to them and handing Susan a folded piece of paper.

'Of you go quick. You're the first couple to sort yourselves out.'

On a window-ledge Neville noticed a flesh-coloured candle shaped like a breast with a wick coming out of the nipple. If it was a clue it was not one he was going to point out to Susan. He looked away but its image lingered in his mind. Ruby Abrams was confronting them, saying to Susan: 'How does he do it? What chicanery! Off with his head!' To Ralph she said accusingly, 'You're saying nothing.'

'I know. It's something I'm good at.'

Susan gave him a push in the direction of the door and they hurried out of the room, going even faster on a joint impulse along the passage so that they ran down the stairs. Susan laughed: 'This is fun. Quite an adventure.' Her nervousness and slightly artificial manner had vanished.

As Neville opened the front door she studied the scrap of paper and whispered: 'I say. First let-down of the evening. "Find Marie – in Berkeley Square?" Do you think Daniel's pet theme could be simply Monopoly?' When she laughed Neville had noticed that her teeth, though very white, were rather uneven; he was always amused by the high standards he expected in other people's physical appearance, standards he certainly could not meet himself. He said: 'After my luck in partners you'll not find me complaining about anything that happens from now on. Particularly as I drew you by cheating. I'm afraid I kept my eyes open and took "Orpheus" because I was too vain to take "Soap".'

'So what! I cheated too.' Susan gave him a look that was frankly coquettish but instead of experiencing pleasure he was mystified by this further turn of events, and nearly exclaimed 'Really?' for the second time that evening.

'Now come on, Rafe,' she said in a passable imitation of Ruby Abrams's voice. 'Don't be so humble! Is it so puzzling that I should choose you as a partner? I have a feeling you will make an excellent detective. Another reason is that I want to hear the end of your story about when you were wounded by that SS man.'

Neville was normally suspicious of his inability to accept a compliment, suspecting it to be a subtle form of egotism – but in these circumstances he knew he was right to be wary of her flattering behaviour. He had achieved the age of forty-five without previously being singled out for such attentions; with Rachel he had made the first move and initiated their early meetings. It must be a hoax, but how could he complain when it meant having such an attractive companion. Replying, he used a slightly cagey tone: 'OK. If we get a few minutes later on I'll tell you. But it's my only war anecdote of interest, over the years it has evolved a strict form and cannot be given in a shortened version. Meanwhile, back in the clue-hunt, what have you got? I'm sure it's some kind of royal theme.'

'Snap again! I've been trying to think of a Queen named Marie. Was there one in Rumania or somewhere like that?'

'There you have me. I don't know about being a good detective but certainly I'm an ignoramus where Kings and Queens are concerned.'

Susan did not reply but tightened her grip on his arm. Seeing her in profile he noticed that her jaw was slightly prognathous, which accounted for the barely perceptible lisp. With her free hand she gestured vaguely towards the end of Charles Street and then said: 'Suppose nothing happens when we get to Berkeley Square? What then? I can well imagine all sorts of things going wrong in a game like this.'

As if on cue a youngish man sprang out from behind a telephone box, dressed in a sort of Ruritanian uniform with a high-crowned peaked cap. The top part of his over-long great-coat was rakishly open to disclose a thin chest much burdened with medals and decorations. He had a handsome slightly weak face and a stage moustache. His manner was suitably dashing. He bowed and clicked his heels. 'Good evening Madame.' He looked pointedly at Susan's Quest badge. 'I believe you have a document for me.'

Susan extended the crumpled scrap of paper directing them to Berkeley Square. The man took this and tore it into pieces, theatrically throwing them into Neville's face as if challenging him to a duel. Then he kissed Susan's hand, gave her another piece of paper, bowed and swung off back along Charles Street. After a few paces he turned round to wave farewell with a poignant smile. Neville said: 'Ah me! *Partir, c'est mourir un peu!* That must be what they call a bravura performance.'

'Poor chap. Fancy having to hang around here dressed up like that. Still I suppose he's an actor "resting". When you think of the organization required in this game, it's no wonder Daniel looked anxious.'

'I know. It's a pity you're seeing him like that because he's usually very relaxed and good fun. After a few drinks a latent talent for mimicry and fooling about emerges.'

Susan exchanged a final wave with the Ruritanian figure and unfolded the other piece of paper. 'Leave Princess Stephanie and fly to the Battersea Fun Fair. Promenade in area before the Old Time Cinema, ride on Big Dipper.' She made a face. 'Big-Dipper – oh dear, I'm not terribly keen on Big Dippers.'

Neville signalled a taxi coming from Bruton Lane. 'Let's get to Battersea first. There's a chance we can solve the puzzle before we get involved with the Big Dipper. Marie and Princess Stephanie – if we can identify them perhaps something will click.'

When they were seated in the taxi Susan said: 'I have a suspicion that Daniel gave us an extra clue in his story about playing Monopoly with that little girl. I can't explain why. Perhaps just the odd way in which the story popped out – as sometimes happens when you don't intend it to, and you say what is at the back of your mind.'

'*Very* good. I thought you had me cast as the detective.' Neville was always interested in the kind of sybilline wisdom which enabled Rachel to sum up a situation irrationally.

Susan looked out of the window: 'Buckingham Palace. Now you have time to tell me about after – after the SS man broke your shoulder, collar-bone and three ribs . . . '

Having his own words sedulously repeated made Neville again wonder whether Susan was making fun of him. She had a serious expression, but possibly she was secretly amused at the way he had dragged the story in to excuse his anger in Lansdowne Row. 'All right. Actually it's a story that I've rarely told. There's absolutely no glory in it for me – I have the invalid part. But I was thinking about it today – it's practically the anniversary of the event, and after all it's the only time someone saved my life. Well, I was there in Vierzon with two other wireless operators. One of them, called Benbow, was shot by the SS lieutenant who came to the house. This lieutenant also floored me, but in turn he was killed by the other operator, a very cool customer named Duff Gordon. There was a big gash in my neck and shoulder – I've got an impressive scar to illustrate this story. The pain was fierce and I passed out. When I came to Gordon had put a dressing on my wound and disposed of the bodies. He buried them in a stagnant pond. He could not move me upstairs so we had some scarey hours waiting there to see if we would have any more SS callers. But they had found quite a pocket of *maquis* and were kept occupied by them till they moved out the next day towards Orleans. Our mission was called off and a Lysander was flown in to pick us up. That was it.'

'And what happened to Duff Gordon? Do you ever see him now?'

'Never seen him since the day we arrived back in England.

I went into hospital, was down-graded medically and didn't return to the same unit. Then after the war the Phantom Signals was one of the few army units not allowed to have reunions by the War Office. I know that sounds absurd but it's true. I wrote Duff a letter while I was in hospital, but there was no reply and so I gave up. I admired him a lot, hero-worship I suppose, that kind of thing, but we were quite different types with very little in common. I know I used to irritate him.'

'How?'

'Lots of ways. I was always whistling what he called "American muck". He was a great fan of the Music Hall songs. Then we argued a lot about the war – he was very cynical about the motives of the nations involved and I was a complete idealist. After all I was only nineteen then.'

Neville looked out to see that they were speeding towards the Ebury Bridge Road. Some trick of light made the sky above the B O A C Air Terminal building appear plum blue. A shadow of a frown had appeared on Susan's face. He pointed at her. 'There, you see, the boredom of my narrative has struck home. I'm sorry.'

'Not at all. I think it's a shame you never got to see this Mr Gordon again. He sounds an interesting character.'

Neville nodded. He had no intention of enlarging further on his mundane army career, and it was not possible to give a portrait of such a complicated character as Duff in a few sentences.

'One other thing I meant to ask you earlier. Why are you here? This is a Monday – shouldn't you be in the country?'

It was like being put through a catechism by a pleasant but firm schoolmistress. He could understand the inquisitions he went through to satisfy Rachel's curiosity, but why Susan Latymer should want much the same kind of information was beyond him. 'My family are having a holiday in Southern Ireland with my wife's sister. They've hired a horse-drawn caravan.' He looked down at the calendar on his watch. 'It's the 13th, so they should be on the road between Ballinspittle and Timoleague Abbey. Clonakilty Bay, somewhere in that area. They'll be having a fine time but it's not my cup of tea. I shall have a seaside holiday with them later.'

'A pity to miss that though. Like Mr Toad's jaunt in "Wind in the Willows" . . . ' She let the sentence peter out and stared out of the window as the taxi sped up to Chelsea Bridge. It appeared that her desire for information about him had been sated.

Mist was rising like a gossamer ribbon from the Thames but the sky above the fanciful outline of the Albert Bridge was free from clouds, so clear and glittering with stars as to seem quite unreal. Neville paid off the taxi in Queenstown Road and they began to walk along the Bridge Drive in silence. In the distance he saw a sign ARCADIA – ADMISSION FREE and drew Susan's attention to it saying, 'I fancy that myself. Should be better than the Big Dipper,' but as they got closer the smaller lights below ARCADIA resolved themselves into MINI TEN PIN BOWLING. Susan said: 'That's life for you. Nothing's quite what it seems.'

As they queued at the turnstile, Neville could feel tiredness seeping into him. It had been a long day, and the emotional ups-and-downs of a meeting with Rachel were more fatiguing than a solid day of work. The drinks he had downed had given him a slight lift but as that wore off he would become a decidedly lacklustre partner for Susan. He began to puzzle his brain strenuously about the identity of the royal Stephanie and Marie.

The carousel calliope played the Beatles' tune 'Michele' as they slowly walked round obeying their instructions. Neville noticed the graceless figure of a man with an ugly hang-jaw face and over-large hands watching them covertly, and expected that he might approach with another clue, but when he looked back the heavily built man had disappeared.

'Nothing for it I'm afraid but the Big Dipper. Unless you don't want to go through with that.'

'Oh no. We'll press on. I can take one of those rides okay but after that I begin to feel queasy.'

There were not many people waiting on the wooden platform where the Big Dipper coaches came to rest. Neville eyed a small Pakistani family and a larger, more vocal, group of teenagers, feeling that perhaps Daniel Priest's organization had broken down and they had come, willy-nilly, to the end of the clue-hunt. But as they took their seats two men hurried in, one of them being the ugly man he had noticed near the entrance.

'This is it. Hold tight – in more ways than one. There's a couple behind us – one of them a man with a miserable expression I noticed before – I bet we are going to be exposed to some further dramatic turn.'

'My God! What can they do up in the air?' Susan's face appeared very pale as it had earlier in the evening. She moved uneasily in the seat as if she had changed her mind about the ride, but it was too late as the coaches were already rumbling along, gathering speed.

Neville turned round to confirm that the men were seated behind them. They looked as if they were in working clothes and might be attendants at the fair. They wore slightly self-conscious expressions.

'Don't worry, Susan. Rely on Daniel. I'm sure he won't have planned anything terrifying . . . '

His sentence was cut off as they went down the first dip. Rushing through the cool night air at such a clip took his breath away momentarily. He put his right arm round Susan's shoulders. 'Shout if you feel like it. It relieves the tension. I may do the odd bit of screaming myself.'

'Help – please help.' The cry uttered behind them was in an extraordinary, falsetto voice. Neville was forced to turn round to find the source of the absurd mock-agonized noise. The two men had assumed masks, one of which was vaguely feminine with strands of long hair attached. Neville tightened his grip on Susan's shoulders to ensure that she did not turn round, waving with his other hand in a futile gesture to assure the men he knew what they were up to and they should carry it out so as not to frighten his companion. The coaches were laboriously making the long pull up to the highest part of the track. The man in the male mask produced a revolver, put it at the head of the other one and pretended to fire, then repeated the action towards himself. The pantomime was just completed before the coaches made the long, swooping descent. This time the helter-skelter movement did force a cry from Susan, a combination of an exclamation, his own name and some blasphemy.

As they sped through a series of lesser dips Neville told Susan that the men had performed their set-piece. 'Supposed to represent a man and a woman being shot. Any ideas?'

'What was that place – where those Habsburgs were killed – you know – it touched off the 1914 war . . . ' The anticlimactic part of the ride was bumpy and prevented Susan from concluding her suggestion till the coaches had come to a halt. 'Sara – Sarajevo – that's the place. It was on the tip of my tongue earlier this evening. Haemophilia was definitely linked up with the Habsburgs, I remember that from a lecture.'

'Sounds a possibility.' Neville watched the two men getting out of the coach and approaching them. The heavily built one came right up and said in a shamefaced way, pointing to the Quest badge: 'Hope you understood all that. We were just following instructions and earning some beer money. All right?'

'Yes, of course.' Neville handed him a 50 pence piece. 'Have a pint or two on us tomorrow.'

'Thanks guv. I've got something for you here.' He examined two slips of paper to check their contents before handing them over to Neville and Susan, saying, 'That's it then guv. Good night.' He ambled away with a slightly rolling gait.

'Emperor Hotel, Old Burlington. To be or not to be?' Susan read out. 'Have you got the same?'

'No, by God, I haven't,' Neville replied in a slightly nettled voice. 'I've got "Ottoman Turkish Baths, Dover Street. Find Mr Mayer". I say, shall we settle for Sarajevo and go back now?'

'There's one weak point about that idea of mine,' Susan said. 'Surely it was a man and his wife who were assassinated at Sarajevo. Do you know their names? I don't, but I can't see how two women were involved. It was Princess Stephanie and Marie, remember.'

'Reluctantly I have to agree. It was an Archduke and his wife. Pity that. I feel about the Turkish Baths much the way you do about Big Dippers. I've never been to one and was hoping to get through life without the experience.'

'Why?'

'Oh, the whole idea just lacks appeal. I've always imagined it to be like the baths after football at school. Distinctly unappetizing from my point of view. However, if you think we should go on . . .'

'Look – it's a quarter past eleven. Let's make this the last call whatever happens. I'll go to the Emperor and you to your delectable Baths and then straight on back to Charles Street. I don't think we can honestly settle for Sarajevo when we've already been supplied with a firm clue in Marie and Stephanie . . . On the other hand you're taking on a decidedly dejected look. We'll give it up if you like.'

Neville stood still, silent for a minute, weighed down by indecision. He felt tired and really did not enjoy the prospect of a Turkish bath. He shrugged, saying, 'Yes, all right, let's go on. After all the trouble Dan's taken it would be feeble to resign now. A taxi can drop me on the corner of Dover Street and then take you on to Old Burlington.'

6

Night. Deep in the constellation of Andromeda there is an awesome object – a faint, candle-shaped star just visible to the naked eye on an exceptionally clear night between Pisces and Cassiopeia. Neville knew that if he kept his head still for a few minutes the details of the ghostly image would imprint themselves on his retina. Yet this seemingly minute thing was the vast Andromeda Galaxy, sister to our own Milky Way system, so far away that its light waves travelling at 186,000 miles per second took two million years to reach us.

Neville stood at the corner of Dover Street and Piccadilly watching the light that beckoned then disappeared as his concentrated gaze was broken. He turned from the fantastic prospect of stars to the elementary representation of a crescent moon that showed the location of the Ottoman Baths. The electric moon was a permanent feature, but the orange sign OTTOMAN BATHS flashed on and off, alternating with others in violet and red: TURKISH & SAUNA – OPEN NIGHT & DAY. To Neville the name of the establishment with its possibly intentional pun, the gimcrack electrical effects and the shabby doorway were equally depressing.

When Neville reluctantly opened the half-glass door engraved with a palm tree he found he was again in a Victorian ambience, but a decidedly seedy one this time, quite different to the slightly run-down elegance of Lady Villiers's home. A potted aspidistra stood on a tripod. There was a high dingy ceiling and a glass chandelier in which the lights did not function, a wall painted dark brown on his right hand and on the other a long counter surmounted by a metal grille Behind the counter there was a bank of lockers and two men, one old and dressed in a dark grey cotton jacket struggling with some intractable object out of sight, and the younger one in a white roll-necked pullover who came forward to greet Neville: 'Evenin', Sir. Spendin' the night, Sir?'

'Well, really I was looking for a Mr Mayer.'

'That's all right then. You're spot on.' The man in the pullover pointed to W. M. Mayer in blue letters on his chest, then noticed Neville's badge: 'Oh we're expectin' you, sir, and to say that a Mr Ling will probably be joinin' us. Well, that's the message we got anyway. A – Mr – Ling.' The repetition was made very slowly as if Neville might prove to be a dull pupil.

Having found Mr Mayer and heard his enigmatic message did not seem to have furthered the clue-hunt one jot, and Neville was forced to the dubious activity of inquiring about a bath. 'I've – actually I've never been to one of these places before. Sorry to sound simple-minded but what does it involve?'

W. M. Mayer did not reply immediately but looked back above his shoulder at a big clock. 'It's a quarter to twelve sir. Normally our gents after twelve are stayin' the night and it's two pound then, early mornin' cup of tea included . . . ' He sensed that Neville was going to be a hard sell where a night stay was concerned, and changed his patter. 'But of course if you want a quick in and out, first time like, we'll take your pound.'

'How long would it take?'

'Naturally that's up to you, sir. Some like to spin it out with a nap. But you *could* be out in forty minutes.'

Neville handed over a pound. 'What do I do now?'

'Don't worry, sir. I'll look after you. Now first . . . ' Mayer slid out a locker. 'All your valuables in here. Watch, money, anything in your pockets.' He went to the end of the counter, bringing the drawer of the locker with him. Below the pullover he wore what looked like jodhpurs. He was a bandy-kneed jockey figure, spare and fit-looking. 'All of them mind. And *this*.' He produced a key on a leather loop. 'Once we've locked the drawer this key goes on your wrist and does not leave it again till you're back here, feeling fresh as a new-born babe.'

'Do you mean I should keep it on even when I'm in the bath?'

Mayer took the drawer containing Neville's watch and cash in silence, handed it over to his older colleague for him to lock, then returned to walk along the corridor with Neville, talking to him like a father. 'As I say, you keep it on *all* the time, sir. These rules are the result of many years of experience and have been made to protect *you* sir, not us. Now the drill is . . . ' He produced a plastic bag and began to speak very slowly, as if to a backward child: 'You take – these two towels. You go – down one floor. You – pick a booth. You undress – and put your coloured towel – round your waist. You go – down another floor. Use – the hot box – or the sauna. After you've – sweated a while – a shower and plunge. Then – repeat the process – if you like. Or ring – and I'll bring you some tea. Right?'

Neville nodded and was anxious to be off but was restrained by Mayer saying: 'Name's Wilf. Just ring if you don't know what's what.'

Neville thanked him and hurried down the first flight of stairs, keen to be the first person ever to complete a Turkish bath in fifteen minutes.

The atmosphere on the second floor was steamy, smelling faintly of sweat and eau-de-cologne. There were about twenty booths, separated by four-foot-high wooden partitions, each containing a bed, chair and steel hangers for clothes. All of the booths appeared to be empty but the beds had been used. He undressed and experimented in tying his coloured towel round his waist, remembering suddenly that he had taken off the key-thong and replacing it guiltily. There was no doubt that he did not have the knack of appearing decently garbed in a towel; each of his attempts ended in achieving a daring slashed-skirt effect. Settling for the least provocative version he looked up to catch sight of himself in a full-length mirror. It was a wholly ludicrous apparition. He jangled his key, blew himself a kiss and said 'Mm – mother buy me *that*' before hearing a stifled exclamation across the room. Lying on a bed there was an aged corpulent man, struggling to get into long pants, watching Neville's exhibition with a mixture of bewilderment and indignation. Clutching his towel-skirt, Neville hurried down the slippery stone steps.

On a blank white wall at a bend in the stairs there was a simplistic design of a naked man and the lettering IS YOUR KEY ON YOUR WRIST? Neville was much relieved to find he had the baths to himself and would be spared the sight of great beefy bottoms. He sang a snatch from the Beatles' song 'Nowhere Man' then explored the chambers which were exuding great clouds of steam. A minute sitting in one of them was enough to convince him that he would not enjoy the sweltering heat. But the plunge looked decidedly inviting, like a small swimming pool. He walked gingerly over the greasily wet stone floor, counted the steps down into the pool to ensure it was reasonably deep, and dived in.

The water was chlorinated but appeared to be surprisingly clean; apart from his eyes stinging a little when he surfaced there was nothing to complain about. The plunge was approximately twenty feet long, descending from five to perhaps ten feet in depth. He swam a few lengths and his weariness ebbed away. Five more minutes swimming, a quick towel down, perhaps a cup of tea brought by the cheerful Wilf Mayer and he should emerge from the Ottoman Baths in better shape than he had expected. He would forget about the mysterious Mr Ling and return quickly to Charles Street in the hope that some Château Grillet remained.

He did an expert duck-dive, one that was too good to waste on an empty pool, and began to swim under water. As he did so the solution to the clue hunt, unsummoned, came to him. MAYER-LING: Mayerling was the name of the castle or place where the Austrian Crown Prince Rudolph had committed suicide with his mistress. Marie must be the name of his mistress and Princess Stephanie would be his partner in an unhappy marriage planned for him by his father, the old Emperor.

'The Lost Chord – I found it! I found The Lost Chord!'

he could hear Schnozzle Durante jubilantly exclaiming, and felt much the same himself. Surprised by the brilliance of his deductions, he nearly chortled under water. When he reached the steps and looked up he saw a man built like a Japanese wrestler sitting at the top of them, smiling down as if he had been admiring the under-water display. Neville began to pull himself up the steps, expecting the gross figure to make way, but instead he walked into a deft left hand blow to the neck that was as jolting as an electric shock.

A suspicion that Turkish Baths attracted a fair percentage of eccentrics and queers had been behind his prejudice against them, but to run into a madman on his first visit seemed fantastically unlucky. He raised his hands to ward off further punches but received another searing forearm blow to the side of the neck which made him stumble, defenceless before a third one delivered as if this mayhem specialist was trying to pole-axe him. Neville recovered his balance and hit the fat man with a vicious left jab, and had the satisfaction of seeing it draw blood, but the strangely feminine mouth remained smiling. His assailant had an antinomian face and very full wavy brown hair growing like a woman's on the low forehead. There was a swallow or swift tattooed on the back of his left hand.

Protesting nerves set off alarms in Neville's head: he was struggling to defend himself but the three savage blows were an impossible handicap as they had blunted his ability to think what he was doing. He was already half out on his feet – in boxing this was a time to cover up and keep moving. Just as the idea of springing backwards come to his rescue a thick powerful arm curled round his neck and he was in a fast embrace. He continued to pummel the fat man's ribs but it was like hitting hard rubber. Dully it came to him that he might be tangling with an emissary of Sydney Mansell's. He thought 'Bad joke' and opened his mouth to say something, but the words did not make sense.

Neville took two more jolting blows to the side of his neck but he continued punching till the fat man changed tactics, grabbing Neville by the throat and slowly forcing him over backwards. Neville felt as if his spine might break – it was like the moment when the dentist's drill hit the nerve – his brain would not accept this affront and rebelled, clamouring for escape. Neville knew that if he called out then it would be like a horse whinnying in fear, so he kept his mouth shut tight. For the second time in his life he felt he was only a few seconds away from death.

Neville struck out desperately at the gross chest to which a yellow cotton shirt was moulded with sweat, but his blows were puny. The fat man had stopped smiling and regarded Neville with a grave self-satisfied air. He said, 'That's it,' and the simple phrase of dismissal became a singular warning.

Now that some signal of weakness had been received the fat man directed his pressure to pushing Neville down into the water. There was an insidious force at work in Neville's brain to give up the struggle, as if it was a hopeless one against some anaesthetic. Confused images danced before his eyes and then resolved themselves into the guileless face of his small son – still separated by years from all deceit and intrigue.

Part Two

'Only we die in earnest, that's no jest.'

Orlando Gibbons

I

Lost in a sea of darkness, like a rock now awash, now emerging clear from the waves, now even deeper under black water, Neville was dimly aware of something else – a far off sound, a whispering voice that he could not break down into words.

The darkness flooding his mind suddenly contracted as in an iris-out, and his eyes focused with difficulty on the elaborate plaster moulding of a high ceiling. He still did not know where he was: the only information that the ceiling gave him was negative, that he was not in his bedroom at Montagu Mews. Gradually what had been gibberish could be interpreted: '. . . tongue nerve sounds an alarm in the third branch of the fifth cranial nerve which then signals the central nervous system. After that it's all systems go! The spinal column stretches. Nerve areas in the pelvic system switch on. The pancreas releases insulin. The sex glands fire into action. And that's just with a kiss!'

The roguish masculine voice stopped on a rising note and a lilting feminine one made a suitable bantering reply: 'Is that so? You seem to be quite an expert on kisses.'

The man said: 'That's just what I am. I'm specializing in osculogy. Should do quite well in Harley Street I think.'

Neville momentarily raised his head, which seemed unnaturally heavy and connected in a painful manner to his body, to see that the speakers were a handsome young doctor and a nurse standing near the foot of his bed. The opposite bed was empty. He was at the end of a hospital ward. His slight movement attracted the attention of the young couple and they moved towards him.

'There you are, you see!' the doctor said in a tone of self-congratulation. 'Nature suggested, indeed dictated a certain duration of sleep for recovery. It's over and hey presto!' He began to address Neville directly – his manner was a little patronizing: 'Well, old chap. How do you feel now? A leetle groggy?'

'My neck aches. Where am I?'

'Hospital – King Street – casualty ward.' The doctor's tone became breezy, as if there were something to gloss over: 'You were involved in an incident in the baths in Dover Street, remember? You took quite a beating. One of the attendants pulled you out of the plunge. You were lucky . . . '

The nurse, a pleasant-looking tall girl with a sharp-featured face, nodded her head vigorously to back up this statement. '*Very* lucky, Mr Neville. You really might have drowned if it hadn't been for . . . ' She pulled a piece of paper from her breast pocket. 'A Mr Mayer. It was he who pulled you out of the water. And insisted on coming with you here in the ambulance. He's been back since with your watch and money.'

The doctor had begun to look bored during this narrative. He made an inconclusive gesture. 'No concussion. No bones broken. You've got some bruising on your cheek and neck.' He leaned forward to touch Neville's large scar. 'But I see you've survived much worse things. A day or two in bed and you'll be feeling fit again. I'll have a word later. In the meantime I'll send those chaps in, Staff. Don't let them stay too long.'

The staff-nurse nodded and watched him go with an affectionate lingering look, then turned her attention to Neville. 'You've had some other visitors but they didn't stay. We told them you were going to be quite all right, just a matter of sleeping off the shock, etcetera. A Mr and Mrs Priest and a Mrs Abrams. Mrs Abrams left a note for you – I've got it on my desk. She told me your wife was away on holiday – fortunately there was no need to worry her, so we did not try to trace her.'

'I'm glad about that,' Neville said quickly, then explained: 'Pointless to worry her, as you said, but also she would be hard to find. She's on a tour in your lovely country. I'm right in thinking you are Irish?'

The nurse gave Neville an amused look. 'You're right, but I've been over here so long I didn't think it showed. Would you care for some tea?'

'Thanks – I'd love some tea. Who are the chaps the doctor mentioned? Who's coming in to see me?'

'Detectives. Two of them. They've been hanging about, anxious to have a word regarding the man who tried to drown you. Apparently the good Mr Mayer hit him very hard with a wet towel to rescue you. Then while he was getting you out of the pool the madman ran off. Are you going to be fit for the questions?'

'Yes, I'm fine now.'

When the nurse had gone Neville closed his eyes. Two sentences insinuated themselves into his mind: 'I don't like my girl friends to have husbands. If she can fool her husband she can fool me.' He could not remember if he had read this or whether someone had said it to him. Now the sly philosophy had a special significance for him. How ironical it would be if he had received a beating at Sydney Mansell's instigation just when it seemed possible that Rachel's attentions were straying again – to a Mr Gerald, surname unknown.

'*I don't like my girl friends to have husbands.*' The sentence was repeated in his mind like a disembodied threat over a telephone, heavy with menace.

Sydney Mansell was tough and unscrupulous; Neville was in no doubt of that. He thought it probable too that Mansell, the self-made man reared in an East End basement, had his own idiosyncratic way of dealing with problems. He could imagine Mansell brooding on his wife's clandestine assignations and deciding to seek some kind of revenge, seeking out the fat man. The mayhem specialist might be one of Mansell's packers, or possibly a porter at the vast warehouse near Liverpool Street station. Rachel had led him there once, to satisfy some odd whim. Borers Passage – that was the place. He had parked his car in Petticoat Lane and they had strolled round the neighbourhood till he had lost his bearings completely. Rachel had stopped abruptly in an alley-way, saying enigmatically, 'Guess whose.'

His fanciful imaginings collapsed like a house of cards. Why should Sydney Mansell resort to such a primitive arrangement? Mansell was a respectable, intelligent businessman, not a member of the Mafia. It was nonsense to imagine he would hire a thug.

'Mr Neville. Are you all right, sir? A few questions? We'll keep it short.'

Neville opened his eyes to see two men, both in their late twenties, standing at the side of his bed. The man who had spoken wore a checked sportscoat with a grey button-down shirt and a striped tie. He had a fresh complexion and a cheerful face. He said, 'I'm Frank Rossiter. Detective-sergeant. This is Detective-sergeant Mellish.' The thin sallow man who was introduced, wearing a dark suit and a black tie, nodded but said nothing. They pulled up chairs and sat down.

Neville said: 'Fire away. That fat chap shouldn't be running round. He's too dangerous to be allowed loose.'

Rossiter rubbed his nose while he considered this for a moment. He had sceptical grey-green eyes. 'That's right, sir. From what I've heard, a right tearaway. Now, we've got your details. Saw your friends earlier and they were very helpful. What I want from you at the moment is a description, full as possible, of this man.'

'Five foot nine or ten. Built like a heavy-weight wrestler. About eighteen stone. Strange, bisexual face with a low, feminine-type hairline. Very thick dark brown wavy hair. Greasy-looking skin. Wore dark grey trousers. Yellow cotton shirt. Rings on both hands.'

'You got the odd detail sir.'

'That's right. It's a kind of hobby with me.'

'Anything else?'

'He had a swallow or swift tattooed on the back of one hand. But I think he is a wrestler. He appeared to be very fat but there was no flab on him. A forty-four inch waistline, but hitting him was like using a sack of wet sand for a punching-bag.'

Mellish examined his nails minutely and Neville wondered what part he was supposed to play in this interrogation.

Rossiter nodded thoughtfully. 'This tallies with what the attendants at the baths said, but you got more details fortunately. You've never seen this man before?'

'Not as far as I'm aware, and he's not someone you'd easily forget. Oh, the other thing – he's got a very sick smile. If you run into him, start punching . . . '

'That's all right, sir. We'll handle him, don't worry. We give as good as we get, you know. Call it a draw, that sort of thing.'

Neville thoughtfully explored his painful cheek with his tongue. 'Sorry about that. I've got two crowned teeth – the result of an old accident. Just checking to see they were still intact. I'm hoping to run into that fat man myself. For a return bout. I think he owes me one . . . '

Rossiter broke in sternly: 'Now look here sir, we have to prevent members of the public demonstrating that they have a flair for melodrama. Vendettas are very definitely out in this country, I'm glad to say. You leave this to the professionals.' He showed the inscrutable Mellish something in his notebook and received a barely perceptible nod.

Rossiter made another brief pencilled note and went on. 'Won't be long now, sir. We understand from your friends that you were going round London on some kind of treasure-hunt game. We were told earlier in the evening that you were involved in an argument with a youngster, a chap who was wearing Hell's Angels clobber. Do you think that could possibly have any connection with what happened later?'

'Shouldn't have thought so. He made some kind of empty threat as he went off. I don't think it meant anything. If it had, he would have needed to follow me all evening to set up what happened later.'

'Good point. Can you describe this young bloke?'

'Not his face. I was too interested in what he was wearing. He had all sorts of Nazi insignia on his jacket. I know there are shops in London which sell that kind of thing. But he had a *Flandern* badge and *Rex Bewegnung* medal – they must be rarish.'

'What sort of medal is that, sir?'

'It was issued only to Belgians, members of the *Wallonie* division who fought for Hitler. Depicts a vertical sword with a pair of crossed rose stems. The *Flandern* badge shows a black lion on a yellow background.'

Rossiter made another note and commented, 'Well, you never stop learning. I didn't know any Belgians were on the German side. I've jotted it down but I think like you it's a blind alley. What do you think, Bill?'

The man in the dark suit murmured 'Non-runner' and made a gesture, the significance of which eluded Neville but obviously prompted Rossiter's next question. He said, in a rather over-casual way, 'Ever been in those baths before, sir?'

Neville was struck by the possibility that the detectives suspected he might be a queer whose proclivities had brought about the assault. This idea nettled him and he meditated for a moment on bringing it out into the open, then thought better of it, saying simply: 'My first and last time. It was just part of the clue-hunt.'

'I see, sir. One last question and I'd like to take this one slowly, then we'll push off. If you've never seen this fat chap before, do you have any idea of what could have – is it just possible that someone else arranged for him to make the attack do you think?'

'No idea – none whatsoever.'

Rossiter sighed. Something in his manner conveyed that he did not accept everything he was told, even by successful antique-dealers with good addresses and wealthy-looking friends. 'Well it does become a fair old puzzle then. You see we don't go much on this idea of the fat man being a nutter. No, frankly I don't go a bundle on that. You see, I mean, he went into that place with trouble on his mind. Wouldn't give the attendants any valuables to put in a locker – told them he hadn't got anything on him. Lucky for you, that. He could easily have handed them a couple of quid and they'd have been happy. But he was too mean to do that, and nothing in the locker made them uneasy. That's why one of them went down later on, just to check up. So – we have Mr Fatman going into those baths. He leaves nothing in the lockers, doesn't strip off in the changing rooms – the attendant informs us that it's strictly against the rules of the place to go down to the third floor clothed and there's a big notice to that effect. I like a neat crime – it has to take shape or I can't follow it. This one only makes sense if there was a plan. So – well I'm sure you can see where that leaves us?'

'I'm not sure that I do.'

'Well sir, if I'm right and you didn't have the extraordinary bad luck to meet up with a nutter who has it in for men taking Turkish baths on a general principle, then it was organized and Mr Fatman was following you round waiting for an opportunity to close with you. And if it was planned, then someone who knows you must have arranged it. Q.E.D. I want you to think about that. Don't you agree, Bill?'

Mellish had been scrutinizing his nails again as if not too concerned with what was being said: on hearing an appeal for his opinion he got up and methodically replaced his chair exactly where it had been. When this was accomplished he approached very close to the bed and leaned over it to look down directly into Neville's eyes. This posture gave him a slightly sinister, threatening aspect. He spoke earnestly, as if urging the renunciation of a bad habit. 'Yes, I do agree, sir. I suggest you search your mind on that point. While you're lying here quiet and undisturbed. I've scribbled our number down here.'

Mellish said good-bye and walked briskly away, but Rossiter lingered. 'Just one last word, sort of postscript. We do need your absolute cooperation as to ideas. But don't try to find Mr Fatman yourself will you sir? We'll have a kind of agreement, eh sir? You leave the villain to us and we'll promise not to sell any *objets d'art.*' He looked meaningfully first at Neville and then at the hospital bed.

The look was obviously intended to imply that Neville would end up in hospital again if he was foolish enough to take action himself, and for a moment Neville had the impulse to say something about his boxing career to the effect that he had been flooring a number of big men when Master Frank Rossiter was reading comics. He also wanted to point out the improbability of the fat man getting a second chance to attack him as he was emerging from a swim. He mentally framed a sentence, but it sounded absurdly boastful so he let it go, nodding rather wearily and closing his eyes.

After his visitors had left, Neville thought carefully about the possibility that someone had engineered the attack. He did not really believe that Sydney Mansell was guilty – there were more sensible and civilized ways of dealing with an adulterer. But who else could possibly hate him so much, to unleash on him that dangerous thug? He realized it was useless to pursue the matter – he simply did not think there was anybody who hated him enough – and was on the point of nodding off when he realized the Irish nurse was putting a cup of tea on his locker. She held out something, saying, 'I thought you might like to read the note your friend Mrs Abrams left with me.'

Neville sat up. The tea was strong and contained sugar which he did not take, but it tasted surprisingly good. Ruby's letter was scrawled in her vigorous, undisciplined hand over two sheets of hospital note-paper.

Dear Ralph,

We three are aghast at this awful business. Poor Dan is feeling very guilty, saying that it happened because of the clue-hunt, but I've been telling him not to be silly as I know you would want me to nail that idea. We shall keep in touch. You are in good hands and Doctor Maguire assures us you should be feeling reasonably OK tomorrow.

Make the speediest of recoveries and have lunch with me as soon as you can. I've been offered a superb orrery made by George Adams – a lot of dollars and cents are involved and I need your expert advice before coming to a decision.

Surprise, surprise, I won the clue-hunt! It was 'Mayerling' – the name of the hunting-lodge or whatever where Crown Prince Rudolph killed his paramour and then committed suicide. You gave me a vital clue in that Beethoven sonata! I back-tracked on it and found out it was the Hammerklavier, dedicated to his namesake the Archduke Rudolph; and there was a photograph of Lord Edmond Villiers shaking hands with Prince R. himself! Like Sherlock Holmes I solved the puzzle without leaving the building or consulting

Doctor Watson. I'm only sorry I didn't do it quicker – for your sake . . .

By the way your fan turned into a Cinderella and ran out on us before midnite. Susan Latymer phoned from the Emperor Hotel to say she had a bad headache, was retiring reluctantly from the clue-hunt, and was going straight home. So! But you still have the fond wishes of

Yours ever

Ruby

Neville smiled as he read the letter. It was typical of Ruby: no doubt she had intended only to show concern and affection, but she could not avoid dragging in a business matter and a little boasting.

A headache – that could well have been the real explanation of Susan's odd glances which he had intercepted during the evening. Neville admitted to being obsessed by the geography of faces; describing it to Frank Rossiter as 'a kind of hobby' had been an understatement. He was also fascinated by all he could learn about what made people tick – what they really thought behind the masks they assumed – noticing the involuntary hostile gesture, and depression masquerading as euphoria. As his interest in the buying and selling of antiques had declined, his fascination with such data about human beings had grown in inverse proportion. But he knew it to be a highly speculative fallible practice.

Ruby Abrams had thought that Susan was looking at him with 'ha ha' eyes while really she had been peering out of the miasma of a headache; he had been similarly led astray by the same symptoms. Nevertheless, finding out the occasions when one had made wrong deductions would not stop him from trying to read human character from tiny signs and obscure messages. Once when he had been lying with Rachel after love-making she had talked at unusual length, weaving an imagined future in which they ran away together, saying at one point: 'We shall have to live cheaply you and I.' A few moments like that, of what seemed genuine simplicity and feeling, had helped to build the picture he hoarded of Rachel against the times when he felt that all she really wanted was any healthy male with a strong sexual drive.

The thought suddenly occurred to him that perhaps he had partly induced the headache for Susan; he knew he was quite a different person than a reader of his book might imagine him to be, since the book preserved all his early enthusiasm for beautiful things. A few months previously something similar had happened when a young antique-dealer had asked to be introduced to him after a country sale in Yorkshire. Standing in a pub at lunch-time, listening to a lot of old stories about battles won and lost in the antiques game, tales in which invariably the narrator was the only person astute enough to recognize that the statue was by Alphonse Mucha, and so on, Neville had felt terribly bored. He had tried to hide this when talking to the young dealer but undoubtedly his disillusion about the business had shown; and he had sensed a faintly antagonistic response.

Ideas were going round and round in his fatigued brain without reaching any conclusion. He had only been awake for half an hour but he felt profoundly tired. He tried to dispel all thoughts of Susan, Rachel, the clue-hunt and his mysterious assailant by calling on his favourite day-dream in which he discovered the perfect uninhabited beach with white sand and deep clear sea. This image brought the accustomed sensation of peace, but as he sank into sleep the word 'perfidious' limped into his mind like an extrovert cripple desperate to attract attention.

2

'Foolishly impulsive,' the Irish nurse Nancy Campbell commented without looking at Neville as she changed down to turn left into Hinde Street. Her manual dexterity extended to gear-changing, and she made the drive in an old Ford 'Popular' into quite a smooth trip. 'And stubborn,' she added as an afterthought. Neville gave his silent assent to these remarks. If she had accused him of being sadistic, pompous, or of having bushy eyebrows he would have objected vigorously, but most other criticisms found their mark in him.

'Dr Maguire said that if you chose to discharge yourself against expert advice there was nothing he could do about it, but anyone with sense would stay another twenty-four hours. So why the rush?'

'Tea very good, coffee not so good,' Neville replied absently. His mind was only partly concerned with his pleasant companion's conversation. He had tried, without success, to remember the Walberswick telephone number that Rachel had given him, and realized that in jokingly turning it into 'Candlestick 999' he had probably destroyed his chances of summoning it back. And where had he put the envelope with the directions to her aunt's cottage? He thought he had transferred it from his dressing-gown to the trousers he was wearing but it was not in the pockets.

'And flippant.'

'No, sorry, that was a poor joke. It's an excellent hospital and I'm sure there's a very good medical reason for making the coffee weak. I've just got a prejudice against hospitals that stems from the only time I was in one. It was during the war – a military hospital with army discipline and so on. Even when we were getting better and were allowed out in funny old blue uniforms we had a regimental sergeant major in charge of us to see we did not go out for eight hours instead of six. That sort of thing. So now the mere smell of a hospital makes me want to escape.'

'Was it really so terrible?'

'Perhaps not. The nurses were very nice. I eventually married one of them. But you definitely got the feeling that the patients were right at the end of a long line of people to be pleased. We had to jump out of bed very early even when we didn't feel much like it to satisfy the almighty doctors, the Sisters and of course Matron.'

Nancy Campbell sniffed – it was obvious she would not go along with any criticism of the medical profession; she seemed to think that Dr Maguire made the sun rise and set. Neville said quickly: 'Don't think I'm not grateful to you and your colleagues. Honestly I have such a high opinion of the place that I think I shall wear a tag saying "In case of accidents please forward to the King Street Hospital, c/o Staff-nurse Nancy Campbell".'

'M-m. All this is being taken down and may be used against you sometime. What was wrong with you in the war – something to do with that big scar?'

'Yes – I had a gash in my throat and it didn't receive proper treatment for about a week. It became infected and I got blood poisoning. My shoulder was broken too, that's why I look a bit lop-sided.'

'I didn't notice.'

'Flatterer! And, as my friends will readily tell you, flattery goes down well with me. But if it isn't flattery then my tailor lies to me – he tells me he has his work cut out to make me appear nearly normal.'

'Rubbish. Perhaps it dips just a fraction – not enough to show.'

'I choose to believe you. Look, won't you come in for some coffee? Good strong coffee.'

'No, but thanks all the same. It's a tempting offer but I do have to meet my friends.'

'What a swindle. Hearing you were going off duty – that was the real reason I insisted on discharging myself.'

'Fool! Will the corner do?'

'Of course. That's fine.'

'And you promise to take it easy, have a day or so of complete rest?'

'Indeed I shall. And frankly I shall sleep better at home in my own bed than in a hospital ward with fifteen other men.'

'That's true. Oh well, 'bye then and good luck.'

'Good-bye. Thanks again.'

Neville waited till she had driven out of sight; on turning away he experienced the exhausted step of someone emerging from a long illness, but this unpleasant sensation had left him by the time he had reached his front door and bent down to collect a bottle of sour-looking milk. Opening the door released an eddy of warm air that had built up behind it during long hours of sunshine.

On the doormat he found one of the ubiquitous circulars from a 24-hour emergency plumbing service and a coloured postcard of Ballycotton Harbour. Picking it up he visualized the little fishing-boats returning in the evening, the man who hawked fish trotting his donkey-cart along the quay, the unimpeded views of sea and sky, and could practically smell the seaweed-tasting air. Some hastily scribbled lines from Helen told him that his family had made slower progress on the caravan tour than expected but were having a fine time. He experienced a brief longing to be with them, sharing simple guiltless pleasures. Once more he was deeply aware of his perverse folly in hazarding all that his family meant to him by his obsession with Rachel. He stood quite still, experiencing a kind of mental tug-of-war, but then the pang of conscience relaxed with a sense of being physically released.

Upstairs he prowled through the small flat, looking round carefully as if he expected to find traces of an intruder, but everything was exactly as he had left it.

With the postcard of Ballycotton propped up on his desk he dialled a phone-number, preparing a suitably breezy voice in case Alida Patterson answered the call.

'Mrs Jackson? It's Ralph Neville. Can I speak to Alida please? Oh well, will you give her a message? Say I had a slight accident and that's why I didn't go to the shop today. I fell down and bruised my face. Tell her I shall not be in tomorrow but I'll phone her later in the day. I want to take it easy in the morning. Underline the fact that it's nothing much – you know what a worrier she is. Many thanks.'

He had been very keen to leave the hospital – indeed, while he was doubtful whether this was possible he had felt like a prisoner without his clothes; but now he experienced a feeling of anti-climax. He fiddled with his cheque-book, thinking of making one out for Wilf Mayer, but could not decide how much to send and pushed it away, beginning instead to open the letters that Alida had handed to him some thirty hours previously. The contents of the first two he opened were exactly what he had expected: a cheque from a museum in Boston and an order for a rare rosewood sympsiesometer made by Joseph Hughes which he had offered to a customer in Versailles. He imagined that the registered letter from the Oxford Street branch of Barclays Bank would contain a foreign draft but he was wrong. The stiff linen-paper container enclosed only another envelope with his name and shop address written on it in a firm large hand he did not recognize. He opened it to find a typed letter and a passport-sized photograph of a man – he stared hard at this for a moment but it was no one he knew. The letter-heading was attractively engraved on a fine cream laid paper:

Strand Close – Strand-on-the-Green – Chiswick W.4

Dear Ralph,

If I address you as young Ralph or say that I remember your Army number was 2602111 then perhaps you'll guess the identity of the writer of this letter. Funny that the only Army numbers I can remember apart from my own are yours and poor Curly's!

Prepare for a shock old chum as there is no way I can spare you that. You see – if you're reading this letter then I'm a dead man. I've arranged with my Bank that they should send it to you three months after my death.

The reason for me writing like this – perhaps you'll find it macabre but it is only like taking out a life insurance policy really – is that I want you to do me a great favour. But first I should tell you why I haven't contacted you before. I'll try to explain . . . You see for some time after the war I couldn't settle down, I pulled off a good stroke of business and didn't need a steady job, I roamed around

Europe, married a Swedish girl and lived in Sweden for some years. When we returned to this country we took a house in rural Essex. It is only for the last three years that we have lived in Chiswick. How did I come to find your address? I spotted your photograph in a magazine when your book on antiques came out and tracked you down then. The reason I didn't call in to see you was that I had this plan in mind by that time. You see I've had a bit of ticker trouble and I asked my doctor for the straight gen. He didn't try to fool me, laid it on the line in fact that one day I might just keel over. So in that event I'm going to need someone to wrap up my business and collect the lump sum in lieu. The trouble is that the business is not strictly legal otherwise I should be leaving it in the hands of my accountant. As it is I have to find someone else . . .

I expect all these plans sound rather out of character. You never had me figured as a belt-and-braces man did you? But things were different when all we owned was in our kit-bags and I didn't have anyone dependent on me.

Perhaps you're asking 'Why me?' Remember Curly's famous catch-phrase 'Why me Corp . . . ?' And that Salamander scheme on Dartmoor when we slept in the snow for a week and Curly kept on forever QSBing and QRMing until you replied in plain language who he should QSO? Still I think it was then and during the special training at Arisaig and at Vierzon that we three found out we were really mates.

Anyway if you are asking 'Why me?' I'll give you three reasons. (1) It has to be someone who won't take no for an answer and will press on regardless if the situation becomes a little dicey. I've never forgotten that brawl in Folkestone when that Polish acrobat tried to tidy up the alley by kicking you out of it and you kept bouncing back like a yo-yo. Remember I nicknamed you Oliver Twist then? (2) I've two partners in this business and neither of them are up to finalizing matters – so it must be someone I can trust all the way. Quite a sum is involved. (3)? You said you owed me a favour.

It is a lot to ask I know. I want you to take any amount you think fair from my share of the divvy to cover your time & expenses but that won't compensate for being involved in something dodgy. If it is too much to ask you then do me a much smaller favour and just destroy my letter. I *think* you'll do the big one for me. We used to depend on each other. Remember?

Yours

Duff

fiat

As he read the letter Neville experienced a shock at learning of Duff Gordon's death in what he did regard as a macabre communication, but he was aware of other feelings too. The fact that Gordon had known of his exact whereabouts for a year without calling in to see him was in effect the biggest snub he could recall, or at least the one he had felt most strongly. But in his view there was no choice about doing what Duff asked; Neville felt moved by a compelling single-mindedness on that point. There was at last a chance to repay the biggest debt of his life; that there was no possibility of his action being known by Duff or acknowledged only added to his determination.

The references in the letter to the Salamander scheme, the special training at Arisaig on the western coast of Inverness and to Curly's 'QSBing and QRMing' took Neville back to what now seemed a remote and unreal world of call signs, megacycles, circuits, triplers, anodes and inductances; a time when he could recognize Benbow's 'fist' in sending morse code as readily as his North Country accent. They had been given the code-word 'fiat' for their aborted operation in France. At the briefing an Intelligence Corps Major had first used it, loftily adding the rough and ready translation 'So be it'. All three of them had reacted to this word differently. The same evening he had looked up the word in a dictionary to find it described as 'a formula of endorsement', 'a command or act of will'. Benbow had seized on it joyfully as being 'fiart', and always pronounced it that way, saying, 'Yes they're quite right about us fiarting. Oh yes, we might just as well fiart as use those little taché-case sets'. But the Major's definition had appealed to Duff Gordon, who had elected to use it in the fatalistic sense of 'What will be, will be' as it fitted in so well with his whole philosophy of life. 'Let's take a chance' was always his immediate response to any tricky situation. The phrase was often on his lips and had led to his nickname 'the Chancer'.

Snapshots of Duff Gordon. His grin, which could appear friendly or distinctly otherwise and was often used to hide his true feelings. The expert card-player, so brilliant at poker that he had returned from the Yugoslavian mission with a kitbag stuffed with dollars won during a brief stop-off in Bari. His inability to refuse a dare which had led to the reckless motor-bike race with the sergeant in charge of the Dispatch Riders. The sergeant, 'Don R', a regular soldier, had driven with great skill, but had been hollowly beaten by Duff whose tactics were simply to wind back the throttle and take a chance on all the blind corners. It was twenty-seven years since Neville had been the pillion-rider on that mad night dash from Aylesbury to Buckingham but he had not forgotten it. A. D. Gordon the thwarted comedian with a vast repertoire of old-time music-hall songs and a few great favourites like 'Burlington Bertie' – 'living on plates of fresh air/So long without food/ I've forgot where my face is . . . ' and 'You can do a lot of things at the seaside/That you can't do in town . . . '

Neville brooded on the photograph that had been enclosed with Duff's letter. It was a nondescript face: Mr John Average with glasses in slightly dated overcoat and hat. He turned it over to see that there was a Biblical reference in faded writing: Job XXIII, 10. He quickly looked up the appropriate quotation: 'He knoweth the way that I take; when he hath tried me, I shall come forth as gold.'

Neville went into his kitchen rather like a sleep-walker to make some coffee, performing the various small tasks automatically. The thinking part of his brain seemed to have been switched off – he felt abnormally tired, dull and insensitive; he would not have been at all surprised on returning to the other room to find that Gordon's letter had been part of a weird dream and did not exist. But when he put the coffee tray on the desk the Barclays Bank envelope, the smaller one, the photograph and two sheets of cream paper all remained as tangible evidence of the strange communication from beyond the grave.

In any circumstances Neville would have found it hard to take in the fact that someone so vital and seemingly indestructible as 'the Chancer' was dead. When the section operating in Yugoslavia returned to England, Neville had overheard the Colonel who had been in charge say of Duff: 'He's the man I should pick to have at my side on a tiger-hunting expedition.' At the battle-training school where Neville had come under fire with live ammunition for the first time, 'Curly' Benbow had done his best to cheer everyone up by producing a Sunday newspaper with the lurid headline, STOP THIS USELESS SLAUGHTER – Mother Asks Why Was My Son Killed? Battle School Revelations . . . but Duff had been scathing about 'soft jessies who couldn't get their fat heads down'.

Duff had voiced idiosyncratic opinions on most subjects, from luck – 'For a man with spirit, good and bad luck are like his right and left hands – he uses them both' – to religion which he dismissed as something he did not need, exulting in a kind of humorous nihilism and quoting Albert Chevalier's adage: 'Wot's the good of hanyfink? – Why – nuffink!'

3

Mortmain, deadhand: Neville remembered a legalistic word, mortmain, that he had once looked up in a dictionary, something to do with statutes of mortmain. Duff Gordon had planned his letter to have a somewhat similar effect to the 'dead man's brake' they used to incorporate in railway engines. Mortmain, deadhand, the words went round and round in his brain as he drove along the Great West Road towards Chiswick and the Strand-on-the-Green address on Gordon's letter-heading. In effect his hand had been grasped by a dead hand.

Neville's will was the simplest the law could devise, a mere formula of two lines leaving all his property to his wife. The idea of making it contain a surprise or revelation was repugnant to him. Similarly he thought any other form of posthumous communication highly suspect and likely to appeal only to a neurotic, but he could see that Gordon's dilemma had probably made the bizarre letter necessary.

Wednesday the 15th of July 1970, the day following Neville's voluntary discharge from hospital, was very warm with the prospect of being much hotter once the sun had dispersed the flimsy remains of a heat haze. The drive through Chelsea and Hammersmith was frustratingly slow, with numerous traffic hold-ups which added to the oppressive sensation of heat as well as giving him ample opportunity to meditate on the deadhand letter. There was something about it that still puzzled him, as if it contained a coded passage to which he did not hold the cipher. The idea nagged at him for most of the time he was driving but he gave it up eventually as being as incapable of explanation as a fleeting mystical experience.

The prospect of being involved by Gordon's last request in a business 'not strictly legal' he did not find unduly disturbing. Assaults on children sickened him and he could not conceive abetting a crime of violence, but generally speaking experience of life had not ennobled him, it had taught him to compromise. In the past he had himself been guilty of income-tax fiddles and of breaking the law over currency restrictions, so that it would be absurdly hypocritical for him to shrink from something similar but on a bigger scale.

Parking his car by some railings practically at the edge of the Thames, Neville got out to find the sun burning down from a cloudless haze-free sky. A narrow path ran along the river past a few shops. There was a village-like atmosphere about Strand-on-the-Green and he could see that once it must have been a very attractive place, but now one was aware of a continuous noise of traffic from the complex of roads to the north and the view was dominated by tall, box-like buildings beyond Kew Bridge. He spied a postman and asked the way to Strand Close.

'Just follow this path past the Boat Club and a pub called the Bull's Head. About a hundred yards after the railway bridge keep your eyes peeled for a finger-post sign pointing to the house. It's a modern place, rather tucked away, lays well back, but you should spot a green tiled roof.'

Neville thanked him and had started to walk along the path when he heard some more directions: 'Oh, I'd forgotten. You can't miss it just now. There's a "For Sale" sign. Watch out for that.'

This additional advice gave Neville pause to think as it seemed to point to a futile journey, and he stopped for a moment to look round at the river. To the south the Thames could be seen flowing under Chiswick Bridge till the curve in the Mortlake area hid the further reaches. Sun glittering on its surface made it appear like glass or polished metal reflecting brilliant flashes of light. He watched a pair of dragonflies in their erratic, zig-zagging flight across a catchment area formed by a barrier of moored yachts, and seagulls lazily performing aerobatics above a small island. He was sweating freely, probably due as much to feeling slightly nervous as to the heat. He took off his light-weight jacket, transferred Gordon's letter from the inside coat pocket to one on his hip, and loosened his tie.

There were two estate agents' placards by the gate of Strand Close to the effect that the house was for sale but could be viewed only by appointment. He caught a glimpse of the white-painted house which appeared to him rather ugly, but it was attractively framed and secluded from the village by a group of elm trees. A neatly trimmed box hedge on his right hand as he walked along the gravel drive kept the garden screened.

Halfway along the hedge he was aware of the sound of someone splashing in a pool. A moment later he heard a girl's voice: 'Is that the laundry? The bag's on the porch seat.'

Neville walked to the end of the hedge and looked back towards the swimming pool, a rather splendid one with a diving-board and a small chute. The girl who had shouted was alone in the pool, doing an expert crawl away from him – the kind of effortless, economical stroke which he could not hope to emulate. He waved and called out: 'No – it's not the laundry. Are you Miss Gordon?'

The girl reached for the edge of the bath with both hands, pulled herself out of the water and half-turned, all in one graceful movement. He felt sure she was Duff Gordon's daughter even before she nodded. She was so slim that the top half of her yellow bikini appeared a matter of formality. He could see she had Duff's periwinkle-blue eyes, but in the matter of genes she had been rather unfortunate in also inheriting his taut face and skimpy hair. She looked rather put out by Neville's question and her reply barely concealed her irritation: 'Oh, is it the house? No good – you can't view without a docket.'

Even without his jacket Neville was sweating a lot. It had been impulsive to think of calling on Mrs Gordon without a preliminary phone-call but he had imagined that a direct approach might be better.

'No – nothing to do with the house. My name's Neville. I

knew your father – a long while ago. I wanted to see your mother. Will that be all right, do you think?'

'Not at the moment anyway as she's out. But she shouldn't be long.' The girl bent down to pick up a man's stainless steel wrist-watch that lay on her towel. 'Should be back within the hour. Do you want to wait? There are some deck-chairs under the trees. Would you like a drink? You do look hot.'

'I know. I got like this driving from the West End. Don't bother about a drink but I appreciate the offer. Many thanks.'

'I've a better idea. Do you like swimming? If so pop in the pool – there are some spare trunks in the cabin.'

A breeze puckered the still surface of the pool, riffling a herring-bone pattern of faultless artistry, then erasing it and making a spreading spider-web effect. The suggestion of a dip was very tempting to Neville, but it seemed absurd to visit the Gordon household on an errand that must have melancholy overtones for Mrs Gordon and then plunge in the pool before he had even met her.

'No, I don't think so, though it's a very nice idea.' He added a defence of his lobster-like appearance: 'It's these absurd clothes that we men get lumbered with in the summer. All right for you girls in minis.'

'Minis? Minis are out. You should know that sort of thing,' the girl said witheringly.

'You sounded rather like your father then.' It was a prime example of his habit of saying something and thinking afterwards. She gave him a funny look and said: 'Well, suit yourself. My name's Elizabeth but I'm called Liz.'

'Ralph. You know, I am sweltering. I think I may take you up on that swimming offer. A very quick dip just to cool off a bit.'

Liz Gordon silently pointed to a wooden chalet. Opening the recently painted door Neville found that there was a changing room with a small wardrobe, a lavatory, washbasin and shower. It was all immaculate, and there was a delicious pine smell lingering in the shower. There were several pairs of swimming-trunks done up in cellophane packets. He changed quickly but when he emerged from the chalet, blinking in the glaring sunlight, the girl had gone.

Neville made his way carefully down the steps of the pool, like an invalid taking a dip at a spa, did a few strokes then turned over on to his back. It was a singularly unathletic performance but his face and neck were still sore. As soon as he felt reasonably cool he climbed out. Liz Gordon had not reappeared, but a black cat walked slowly across the lawn and then sat down to keep watch on him.

As he put on his clothes Neville was speculating about the value of the house. He had no expert knowledge, but thought that a large place with a pool in a desirable position close to the Thames was bound to be worth twenty-five or thirty thousand pounds. Duff Gordon must have found a very profitable business.

The hand-basin and the taps gleamed as if they had just been cleaned that morning. There was not a speck of dirt in sight but on closer inspection he noticed two tiny printed stickers: one reading 'Wet paint' was stuck on the slatted wood seat, and another adhered to the mirror with a 'Hello gruesome!' greeting.

He left the chalet for the second time, feeling much refreshed and less anxious about what might be a rather tricky interview. He took a deck-chair facing away from the house and was pleased when the black cat came quite close before sitting down again, staring at him intently with calm yellow eyes. Neville lay back in the deck-chair, idly watching the agitated tops of elm trees with a pleasantly relaxed sensation. He held out his hand and the black cat walked to and fro underneath it, purring and arching its back so as to just brush his fingers.

There was a sound of tinkling glasses and Neville looked round to see that Liz Gordon, wearing a short green towelling gown and carrying a tray, was approaching with the careful step of someone intent on not spilling the contents of a full jug. He sprang up saying: 'I say! What a welcome sound. I feel very fortunate. A super bathe and now this. And your cat seems to like me.'

Liz Gordon, putting the tray down, said: 'Gi' us a gottle o' geer guvnor,' sounding like a ventriloquist and lolling her head to appear like a dummy. It was just the sort of thing that Duff Gordon used to do, and it gave Neville a funny feeling to see the gift for mimicry reproduced so exactly in Duff's daughter.

She gave him a direct look. 'I've never seen you before, have I? When was it you knew Daddy?'

'Many years ago. I was in the army with him. From the spring of 1943 to the summer of '44.'

'But you've seen him since then surely?'

'Not once. I did try, by writing a letter. It's a bit complicated, why we didn't ever get together. According to my calculations you may have been born in Sweden – is that right?'

'You're right.' She concentrated for a moment on pouring out two glasses of lemonade. When she looked up she was frowning slightly as if perplexed. 'You haven't heard from Daddy since 1944, yet you knew he was dead. Did you see it in the papers? They rather splashed that "Shivering Sand" business and some of them went to town on the War Office aspect.'

'Shivering Sand? I'm afraid I don't follow you.'

She sighed as she handed him a glass. 'Where he was drowned.' She grimaced. 'Or where his boat went down rather.'

'Drowned? I didn't know that. I just heard he was dead and presumed . . . Good God! What a shock for you and your mother.'

She sipped some lemonade and appeared to contemplate many matters before replying. 'Well, if you knew Daddy you will know he was always one for taking risks. True, he should not have been sailing in that area – it's prohibited as they use it for gunnery practice. But the slowness at getting a search organized because of the bloody War Office – that made matters worse. It was just the same when those youths went wild-fowling and got lost. They've never recovered some of their bodies you know. Did you read about that?'

'No. I'm afraid I don't even know where "Shivering Sand" is.'

'The Foulness and Maplin Sands firing area, beyond Southend and Shoeburyness. We used to live there. Just past them you come to the mouth of the River Crouch and we lived at a village called Burnham-on-Crouch. It's a dangerous place for sailing, what with the sand-banks which are constantly moving, strong currents, tricky tides, wrecks, and also it can be blotted out by fog quite suddenly. Some young men went wild-fowling there a year or so ago and were lost when a sea mist came in like that. Much of that area is prohibited to the public, being War Department property, and that made a search for them very difficult. Fact is some of them just weren't found.'

'And your father went sailing there?'

'Yes. Not for the first time of course. My Mama used to say that a notice saying no was like a red rag to a bull where Daddy was concerned. I've been there with him quite often. Fishermans Gat, Knock John, Barrow Deep – Daddy knew those places like most Londoners know Oxford Street . . . ' She shrugged. 'But that didn't make it safe, of course. On all the maps they stress "much wreckage". Then in April there was this terrible storm, and he was out in a new boat. A small job. When they finally did get down to searching for him, after about forty-eight hours, they found the boat wrecked on the Shivering Sand. His body wasn't washed up for another twelve days, south of there, at a place called Middle.'

She got out of the deck-chair and walked up and down as if movement might relax some inner tension. Then she held up her thin wrist to display the man's watch he had noticed earlier.

'In two weeks the crabs had made quite a mess of him, but his waterproof Omega Seamaster de Ville was still in fine state! How's that for an advert.' She shook her head. 'Sorry if I sound silly or bitter but . . . ' She raised her chin as Duff used to do in an argument and her eyes blazed with indignation. 'But the whole thing about that damn place is so absurd. I mean, if there hadn't been those complications regarding the search he *might* have been saved. Stupid old War Office! Talk about always preparing for the war before the last! There's all this business about a four minute warning and how the Russians could demolish us at one fell swoop, and the War Office is still making preparations to fight the Boer War by keeping that area shut off just to fire their ancient pop-guns.'

She slumped down into her chair again, her eyes smouldering, saying ruminatively, more to herself than to Neville: 'Yes, I am bitter. Very bitter.' Her bobbed hair which had looked tawny when it was wet from swimming was beginning to dry out and show its true blonde colour. Its texture was very fine, like a young child's, and delightful curls were also being revealed by the drying process. Neville could see that her shadowed eyes had dealt with long draughts of unhappiness. She was the sensitive, thoughtful kind of girl with whom he easily found a feeling of sympathy. He searched his mind desperately for some means of cheering her up even to a very minor extent. He tried out a small calibre smile but she was too absorbed in her thoughts to notice him.

When she did turn to look at him, she said: 'Sorry to be such a gloom merchant. But it's – well everything. We're quite broke, you see. It appears that Daddy used to spend every penny he made. That's why the house is up for sale. I love it here, but we've just got to move and that's that. There's a whacking great mortgage on the place, so it means we'll probably go into a rotten little flat. It's no good planning, is it? – things don't work out.'

She bent down to pick up the cat and cradled it lovingly. 'Funny thing is I didn't have any say at all in choosing this house. It was simply the result of a compromise between Daddy wanting somewhere on the Thames where he could keep a boat and Mummy wanting to be within half-an-hour of the bright lights of London. I was staying in Stockholm with my grandparents when the move was accomplished. But as it happened I liked it best. It just suits you and me Tig, doesn't it?' She adressed the last remark to the cat, fondling its head.

Neville knew he was 'foolishly impulsive', as he had been labelled by the nurse: indeed, acting on impulse was a continual factor in his life and one that had paid off reasonably well in his business career. But he was not impulsive enough to hint to the girl that he might possibly be able to help the family's finances by collecting a debt for them. He had presumed that, having agreed to do the favour for Duff, he was expected to contact Mrs Gordon and find out what it involved; but he intended to broach the matter discreetly in case his deductions proved wrong.

Simultaneously they heard the far-off faint ringing of a telephone and Liz got up, depositing the unprotesting Tig like a warm bundle into Neville's lap. As she ran off she gave him the first smile he had seen that morning, and a tiny wave of the hand which he was pleased to receive.

He was thinking about her father's apparent passion for sailing, about which he had known nothing, when she returned. She smiled again as she said: 'That was my Mama. Held up and won't be back till half-past one or twoish. I didn't say anything about you being here as I didn't want to commit you to waiting. But if you care to stay I'll make a snack we can peck at out here. Very simple mind you – lettuce, the odd radish and so on. What Daddy used to call "rabbit food".' She grinned.

Neville nodded: the phrase summoned back one of Duff's favourite Harry Champion songs: 'Don't live like vegetarians/On stuff they give to rabbits/From morn to night/Blow out your kite/On boiled beef and carrots . . . ' He didn't disguise his pleasure in accepting the invitation. 'Fine by me, if it's not too much trouble. I'm essentially a picnic man. Alfresco meals are always the ones I enjoy most.'

4

Duff Gordon's study was set out like a naval operations planning room. One wall was largely covered with maps and charts, another decorated with photographs and detailed drawings of boats. Several charts were photographed, 'blown-up' versions annotated in green ink with courses plotted on them in red lines. There were a few books and magazines on some white shelves but the room had a very practical, business-like appearance, with a group of grey steel filing-cabinets, a radio transceiver on a metal-topped bench, a typewriter on a small desk and two small chairs. There was a large Scandinavian-looking desk consisting of a plain block of wood supported on stainless steel legs: this was bare apart from a telephone and a glass paper-weight. One black leather armchair was placed by the window to command a view of the river.

Neville had been invited into the study by Liz Gordon, who had suggested he might like to look round it while she prepared their picnic, but he still experienced the sensation of being an intruder as he prowled about the dead man's room. This feeling contended with his highly developed sense of curiosity which drove him to scrutinize some of the charts as if he was studying them for evidence. He knew nothing about navigation, but he was intrigued to find that two of them covered the area Liz had mentioned and contained all the names she had reeled off. The 'blown-up' chart of the area just by the Maplin Sands was very heavily annotated. It appeared to his unpractised eye an extremely difficult area for anyone to use for sailing, for apart from the prohibition, 'Experimental firing is carried out on the Maplin and Foulness Sands in the area bounded by pecked lines, and takes place very frequently under all conditions of weather and tide . . . ', it also seemed to be full of tiny sand-banks and patches of very shallow water, and there were apparently other obstacles marked by blue crosses which he could not interpret. After some minutes of searching he found the place-name 'Shivering Sand' cheek by jowl with the designation 'Wreck' and 'Flew sec. bell'. A mile or so away, as he judged it, beyond the Princes Channel, there was a great patch of sea without any obstacles to sailing, and Duff Gordon's habit of plotting courses through Barrow Deep and West Swin appeared extraordinarily perverse.

The charts were really intended to make sense only to yachtsmen who had been taught navigation, and he turned his attention to the one map that had been put up for its decorative aspect, Blaeuw's World Atlas, published in Amsterdam in 1645, with sea-monsters popping up by the 'Terra Australis Incognita' and charming cartouches showing gods and goddesses ringing the world.

Examining the 'Sommerkamp FT-250 Transceiver' and reading the manual ('The designer has avoided using the PA tank as the RX input – he has used proper r.f. coils of optimum design. If you think about it, a Pi net by itself makes a pretty poor RX input . . . ') whisked Neville back once again to the short period when such a specialized vocabulary had not only made sense to him, but was the most important part of his life. Before they had set off for Vierzon poor Curly had spent hours checking up that he knew everything that was essential about the 'little taché-case sets'. He was surprised that Duff Gordon had retained an interest in wireless to the extent of becoming a 'ham'. By the transceiver there was a type-written list of other 'hams', including XT2AA in the Upper Volta, USSR, with whom Duff had apparently exchanged messages.

Neville moved to the desk and picked up the paper-weight to discover that it was one of the unusual Clichy flat bouquet kind with flowers set above a white latticinio basket ground – he knew enough about the subject to be aware that this was rare and valuable. Lifting the paper-weight had disclosed a scrap of paper with some words written on it in green ink. He caught the name Neville and then saw his two London addresses, with a note to the effect that St Christopher's Place was located off Wigmore Street. The addresses were in a pointed, slanting hand that he took to be feminine.

'Such as it is, it's ready,' Liz Gordon called out and then looked into the room. 'Not that there's any danger of it getting cold.' She stared round the room as if it was one she was not familiar with, then walked towards a wall. 'That beauty was ours once.' She pointed to a photograph and a magazine cutting by the side of it. Neville moved to her side so that he could read the sale description of the boat: ' "Hand of Chance". 11 ton Aux Mast Head Sloop Built 1962 by Meeusen, Breskens, Holland. Built of Iroko on steel frames. 5 Ratsey & 1 Sea-horse sails . . .'

'What happened to it?'

'Daddy sold it last year.' She paused, then said, 'My Mama . . . ' and paused again. The isolated phrase became a muffled *cri-de-cœur,* and for a moment Neville expected to be on the receiving-end of some youthful confidence; but it was quite obvious that she changed her mind, finishing the sentence lamely: 'Her name's Karin. She'll be glad to see you. I think she feels that Daddy's friends have dropped us . . . ' Again he was convinced that she had hesitated about adding something else and thought better of it.

She looked very young and vulnerable. He wished that he had got to know her under happier circumstances. Joining the Army when he was seventeen and never having returned to live in his parents' home, together with the fact that they were a happy couple, he had not experienced any emotional ups and downs to do with them such as he somehow imagined might have happened with Liz. Neville's recollections of Duff Gordon were not uncritical enough to have erased the memory of his dangerous temper.

Liz led the way downstairs to collect their picnic and, following immediately behind her, Neville was struck again by her extreme thinness. He knew that it was fashionable for young girls to appear half-starved but he felt that she had overdone it.

'When I knew your Dad he often talked about the kind of food he was looking forward to after the war. Pork sausages, steak and kidney pies, Yorkshire puddings. You're so slim, I don't think it can have materialized. Not,' he added, bending down to pick up the picnic tray, 'that I don't appreciate delicious salads and orange juice myself.'

'I eat masses,' Liz said. 'Even if I wanted to put on weight I don't think I could. But tell me more about the time when you knew Daddy. I was going to ask about that. What was he like then? In 1944 he would have been twenty-six. You'd have been much younger surely.'

'Seven years.' He waited until they were seated before continuing. 'I learnt a tremendous amount from your father. He was rather a legendary figure in our unit. He took part in the Canadian landing at Dieppe in 1942 and had a very exciting time behind the lines in Yugoslavia. Whereas I . . . Well, I went straight into the Army from school. I'd been considered very good at games, won quite a few tiny cups for boxing, that sort of thing. The result was I was very conceited and spoilt. I needed to have all that knocked out of me.'

'And Daddy knocked it out for you?'

'No, that was done quickly by other people, earlier on in my Army career. It was all over with by the time I met your father. He began my real education. Impossible to tell you how much I picked up from him – I didn't realize it at the time of course. How to get on with people, how to make the best of things, how to survive. He was an expert in all those subjects. When to gamble a little and when "to play from a complete Yarborough" as he put it. Then again he never took himself too seriously – could always make us laugh . . . '

Liz looked up suddenly at the sound of a car swirling round in the gravel behind the box-hedge. 'That'll be Mama now.' A shadow passed across her face as if something pleasant was finished.

Neville had started to get out of his deck-chair when he heard a feminine voice calling out loudly: 'Mark my words there'll be tears before the day is done . . . ' This bantering remark tailed off as the approaching woman took in Neville's face. There was a slight accent to reveal that she was not British.

'Mummy took you for a boy friend of mine,' Liz explained quickly as she got up. 'Mummy, this is Ralph Neville. He knew Daddy years ago, during the war, and wants to meet you. We were just going to have a little snack while we waited for you to come back.'

Karin Gordon was disconcerted and it showed, both in her face and in an involuntary gesture as if she was rejecting something. She said, 'Mr Neville,' nervously in a loud voice, giving the impression that she needed time to think. She looked hot and flustered. 'Ralph Neville,' she repeated doubtfully, as if it was the brand name of some dubious product.

At a distance her slim figure and thick blonde hair could have belonged to a girl of twenty, but this illusion vanished at close quarters: on seeing her face Neville judged her to be about fifty. It was a selfish face, corrupted by years of wanting things and then being disappointed with them.

Rather slowly she extended her hand, saying, 'How do you do Mr Neville,' and giving him the kind of thin, faintly disapproving smile he had sometimes seen used by head-waiters. 'Now please don't let me disturb your meal – please.'

'We hadn't started,' Liz assured her. 'I was keeping Ralph far too busy chatting. Look, I'll take the tray back and fill up another plate with the same mixture.'

Liz whisked the tray away. Karin Gordon looked first as if she wanted to object, making another gesture of dismissal, then upset at being left alone with Neville. She appeared to be in a bad state of nerves, restless and irritable.

'I'm sorry about barging in here . . . ' Neville began a rather faltering explanation. 'I called about eleven-thirty and Liz very kindly suggested that I should stay on . . . ' What could have been easy became difficult under a slightly hostile gaze. He realized that she was possibly the kind of woman in whom a latent neuroticism begins to show in over-loud exclamations and involuntary gestures. 'Did Duff ever mention me – my name?'

'I don't think so.' Karin Gordon pondered the matter as though called on to choose between her money and her life. Her noticeable jowls gave her the faint look of a bulldog. She put a beautifully manicured hand to her brow. Neville could tell that she was pulling herself under control, like someone under the influence of alcohol trying to hide its effect. She touched his arm. 'Sorry not to be more welcoming. It's this heat. The humidity rather. What I need is a drink. Let's go inside a minute shall we?'

As they entered the large living-room, which had picture windows looking out on to the lawn and the pool, Karin Gordon gave him a smile that had more feeling in it than the previous one, but still had overtones of artifice. 'I'll just pop in the kitchen a minute and see what's going on, and pour myself a drink. Will you join me? Something stronger than fruit-juice I mean.'

'No, thanks. The orange will be fine.'

As Neville waited for Karin Gordon to re-appear from the door which led to the kitchen, he looked about the room. The house was too immaculate to appear comfortable; he liked things to be reasonably tidy, but the effect achieved in Strand Close was the result of some psychological compulsion. There was not a book, newspaper or magazine to be seen. Everything on view, from the hardwood stairs cantilevered from a centre pole of laminated wood to the low glass table and jade green chairs, looked brand new.

'On a table. With knives and forks,' Karin Gordon said over her shoulder peremptorily as she came back carrying a tray with glasses, ice, and bottles of gin and tonic water. 'I've just told the dear child it would be more civilized to have our meal inside rather than juggling with it in deck-chairs. Do let me give you one of these. With lots of ice.'

He suspected that she had already had a stiff drink. Something had transformed her manner. The nervousness and bad temper had been swapped for rather blatant coquetry.

He nodded his acceptance of the drink since it was already

poured, and she came towards him holding it out in a way that focused his attention on her smooth and surprisingly plump white hand. She gave him a look from head to toe which she knew would not be missed. In this mood she had the attractiveness of a woman who, like Rachel, really knows what she enjoys – in bed. He could see it though he was immune to her charm. Her trick of putting on a different persona, like a quick change artist, had him puzzled, but he was more mystified about the reasons that lay behind this strange behaviour.

'While the feast is prepared let's go through to my little room. Tiled floor and faces north. Deliciously cool at the moment. Sorry again about how I must have seemed just now. Hearing suddenly that you had been Duff's friend – it upset me.'

Neville reflected that it was possible his attempt to read her character had been wrong – perhaps her gestures betrayed only a fundamental anguish.

They went into a room that was shut off from the sun. She stood very close and clinked her glass against his. She had large eyes flecked with gold. Before the lines of dissatisfaction had set in round her mouth she would have been attractive in this aggressively sexy mood. She swallowed and showed him an empty glass. 'Sunk without a trace,' she said, smiling. Duff Gordon's taste in women had always been for blondes 'with some spirit – good for a fight or a bit of the other'. It seemed that he had found the right one to marry.

She sat down in one of the low cane chairs, exposing a lot of her slim white legs. 'Talk to me about when you knew Duff. Perhaps he did mention you and I've just forgotten. It may come back.'

'I knew him a long while ago but I thought he could have mentioned my name fairly recently – in the last year perhaps?' She might not have been the one to write his name down on the slip under the paper-weight, but could anyone so meticulous about cleaning have overlooked it?

Karin Gordon eyed him calmly. She was now in full control of herself and her present situation. She exuded a positive, rather dominating personality. She stared first at the bubbles in her glass and then at his mouth, shifting in her chair so that more white thigh was disclosed. Minis might be 'out' as Liz had declared, but her mother was still wearing them effectively.

'No – I'm pretty sure not. Did you see him in London since we've been living here or was it during our stint at God-forsaken Burnham?'

'I haven't seen him since the war. 1944 in fact.'

She gave the impression of suppressing a mental quiver of laughter. 'But why not? If you got on together, if you liked him? Did you like him?'

'Yes. Admired him too. I can't explain exactly why we didn't meet. Of course he was abroad just after the war, and then I was living in the west of England for some years . . . I don't know really.'

'That was a pity. Duff didn't have many friends.' She looked cleverly at Neville as if trying to convey something more than she had put into words. He felt that it was necessary to say something about the deadhand letter but was determined to keep it vague: 'Well, frankly I'm puzzled . . . The fact is that some time ago I received a letter which gave the impression that I might be able to help . . . Collecting some money and winding up a business, something like that.'

She stared at him calmly again, but he thought he detected some gleeful malignance in her eyes. 'You mean, I suppose, in the event of his death. He wanted you then to collect the money – for us, for the estate?'

'That was my impression.'

'Do you have the letter?'

'Yes, somewhere. I thought at least I should see you.'

'That would imply there was something odd about the debt surely? I mean, ordinary business debts would be collected quite normally in winding up the estate, and so-called "bad" ones could be sent to a debt collection agency. So presumably you suspected there was something dodgy about the business – and yet you were still willing to do it? Why should you?'

'I'm very much in his debt. Something he did for me in the war.'

'I see . . . ' She lingered on this phrase, smiled sympathetically and leaned forward, putting down her glass. 'Trouble is that Duff's affairs were not only complicated but in a terrible mess. He had this strange passion for starting new limited companies. Once he found out how easily it could be done there was no stopping him. And he kept all the reins in his hands, so to speak. You know what I mean. Really, he was like a juggler with so many balls in the air one didn't know which were important, or where the money came from in fact. That was fine, of course, while he was around to do it. But now we're in a horrid muddle. And to be honest . . . ' She leaned forward confidentially, as if even tucked away in the little room they still might be overheard. 'Quite frankly, just between us, I don't think he told his accountant everything.'

She absent-mindedly outlined her lips with a finger-tip as she brooded on this. 'Jamie Woodhouse!' she exclaimed, as if that name was an abracadabra.

'Who?'

'Sorry! Sorry. Thinking aloud. Our solicitor, Jamie Woodhouse, of Woodhouse, Pearce, in Suffolk Street. Do you know it? Near Pall Mall. He's our solicitor, but also a close friend. As I'm sure you are going to be, Ralph.' She held out her hand. When he took it her finger-tips moved sensuously on the back of his hand. She licked her lips before smiling, and once more there was the hint of sexual mischief. 'Give me back my hand this minute and I'll phone Jamie.'

She went through into the living-room and in a minute Neville heard her say: 'Hello Jamie. I have a Mr Ralph Neville here. Yes, Ralph Neville. An old friend of Duff's. On a business matter. Important. Can you see him do you think? This morning? Oh good. Yes, I definitely think you two should have a chat. Most important. Many thanks, Jamie. Very grateful. 'Bye for now.'

5

Suffolk Street is a quiet London back-water, tucked away between the Haymarket and Pall Mall East. It is a cul-de-sac, and as such is comparatively traffic-free, despite being only a few minutes' walk from Piccadilly Circus and Trafalgar Square. Designed mainly by John Nash and George Ledwell Taylor, circa 1820, its yellow stucco has a delightful formal effect without a formal design, like a gentleman's agreement, which may have helped it to attract members of the legal profession. Once it housed Garland's Hotel, an interesting relic of Victorian London, but now it is largely an enclave of solicitors.

Ralph Neville approached it by hurrying down Suffolk Place, and the swaggering Doric ground-floor columns there took his eye for a moment, as did the charming back elevation of Nash's Haymarket Theatre with its series of oval windows stretched across the top. The premises of Woodhouse, Pearce & Co. faced the back entrance of the theatre: they were shabbier than their neighbours.

The hall-way was painted dark green and contrived to look slightly gloomy despite the brilliant sunshine just outside the front door. It served as a reception area for the clients of Messrs Woodhouse, Pearce & Co., whose offices occupied only the ground floor. A mouse-like woman, in a grey dress, took Neville's name with an air of mild complaint, murmuring something about 'Mr Woodhouse – believe – waiting for you.'

Neville sat down on an oak bench without any sense of angst: after a hasty lunch at Strand Close he had driven back to the West End as quickly as possible, and then had luck in finding a parking space in St James's Square; it would have been difficult to clip many minutes off his time for the trip.

Motes of dust appeared particularly heavy in their slow dance in a shaft of sunlight from a narrow window. There was a very faint smell of cooking, something involving onions, so that the air seemed second-hand, as if it had already been used at a café. Otherwise the atmosphere was much like that in an old-fashioned dentist's establishment, with the handful of dog-eared magazines on a table and a job lot of steel engravings to decorate the walls.

The secretary figure did not appear again, but a door towards the end of the hall-way opened and a tall thin man with glasses looked out myopically: 'Neville? – oh, do come in.'

Neville walked into a large room, again very dim, with one window partly obscured by piles of calf-bound books on the ledge.

'Take this chair. Relatively comfortable . . .'

A stagey, loud clock on the mantelpiece began to chime; it took its time announcing that it was three o'clock. Woodhouse waited for it to end, like an amateur actor anxious that not a word should be lost.

When he did begin it was a lot of rather irritating drawling and hesitation: 'Positively Hogarthian – the squalor in which we work. If you run your finger – along a shelf – you'll know it's been there – but I suppose it adds to the appropriate image – of venerable age and respectability . . . ' He had an unhealthy pallor but looked scrupulously groomed, with a parting to his straight dark brown hair which could have been ruled. He wore a black suit, white shirt and a drably striped tie. His thick glasses appeared like one-way mirrors so that Neville had no idea what colour his eyes might be.

'It was kind of you to see me at such short notice,' Neville said. He was in the difficult position of not knowing which cards to play – it was the kind of set-up that Duff would have enjoyed.

'Think nothing of it. Mrs Gordon – friend as much as client. And she's not a *femme sole.* I mean her financial position is not too good – to be blunt. If she can be helped – in any way . . . Tell me – what's your connection in this business?'

'My only interest is to help the Gordon family – if I can. I want to do that very much. The fact is I had a letter from Duff Gordon implying I might be able to do that, with regard to some business of his – in the event of his death.'

Woodhouse was doodling on a small note-pad, carefully drawing an outline of a fat man with pince-nez and a gaping mouth. He said quietly: 'Reasons. Reasons have their reasons. And so on – ad infinitum.'

Neville said, 'Sorry. I don't follow.'

There was some fussy, fiddling pronation of bony wrists in gleaming shirt-cuffs. 'I mean that – here we have Mrs Gordon – recently widowed, and – in none too good a financial position. You suddenly appear – quite out of the blue – someone she has never met – and yet you have your good reasons for putting your time – at her disposal if there – should prove to be – some way of helping her.'

'Yes, that's the position.' Neville looked at Woodhouse to see that his attention was concentrated minutely on the drawing to which he was adding a hangman's noose, then glanced round the room. On the mantelpiece by the side of the chiming clock there was a bust of Dante. The only wall decoration was a reproduction of Breughel's 'The Triumph of Death' showing human victims being shoo'd, beaten and spiked into enormous, devilish bird traps.

Woodhouse crumpled the drawing and threw it into a waste-paper basket. From a desk drawer he took out three thick card-files. 'These are the Gordon dossiers. For the time being – I have all the papers from his accountant – everything relating to the estate in fact.' He made a steeple of his fingers and looked over them at Neville with a faint mocking smile. His black suit and immaculate white shirt added to the impression of a Jesuit priest calmly assenting to a heretic's torture.

'Did the letter give any idea of which business? I choose my words carefully – alas! – Duff Gordon had so many.'

'No – the letter was vague. I suppose that he had deliberately left it like that in case I couldn't or wouldn't help.'

'I see. Alas! We are in difficulties then.' Woodhouse flapped the files down on his desk. 'A veritable mine – of possibly fascinating information. His accountant spent weeks solidly on them – but unusual patience will be required – I'm afraid – to extract some logic – from this farrago of facts and figures. Unexplained sums. And so on and so forth,' he drawled wearily.

'What kind of business was Duff involved in? Mrs Gordon was rather vague too. She said he speculated in various things.'

'Alas.' Woodhouse seemed fond of this stylized expression of regret which meant little if anything. 'Indeed, she was right there. His speculations covered – a very wide spectrum. That is one of our problems. For instance, he did some trading – in commodity futures . . . Are you among the great uninitiated? Ah, well, this involves speculating – as to the future trends of commodities. Say you think the price of cocoa – will rise briskly by next spring for example. You might buy a "lot" of five ton now – for delivery at perhaps £350 a ton. Then if you are right in your reasoning – and the price goes up – you can double your money. If it goes down then, of course – well, goodbyee, don't sighee. So to speak.'

Neville was going to object that the 'business' Duff had mentioned could not possibly be of this kind, but Woodhouse's obscured eyes were fixed on the files and he continued talking as if close concentration on detail might avoid some kind of crisis. 'He even dealt in death. There is a firm in the City – Foster and Cranfield – which holds a monthly auction of "lives" – at the London Auction Mart – in Queen Victoria Street. Buying reversions. It works like this. Mr Y leaves his fortune of £10,000 – to his wife Mrs Y – on the understanding that – she will receive only the income on that sum till her death – when the capital will pass to their son Master Y. But Master Y – he wants some tin now – so he gets Messrs Foster and Cranfield – to auction The Absolute Reversion Receivable Upon The Decease of A Lady Aged – say – 70 . . .'

The lecture was reasonably interesting but it appeared as

if it might be endless. Neville broke in: 'Not that kind of business, I'm sure. Frankly, I got the impression it was something dodgy. That some bending of the law had been involved.'

Woodhouse looked interested but not shocked. He took off his glasses to rub his deep-set, cloudy brown eyes. It was like removing a mask to reveal an essentially cold and humourless visage. 'Alas, alas! – I'm not altogether surprised. I understand that – you were a good friend of Duff's. I like to think I was too. He was a very lively personality. Always managing to engender – an obscure sense of excitement. But I must admit to – a few reservations. Let me show you something.' He replaced his glasses and selected a book from a small open-fronted bookcase behind him. 'Yes – a rare species of homo-sapiens. Read this. It's Macneile Dixon's *The Human Situation*.'

Neville took the book and read the passage that Woodhouse indicated with a long, filbert-shaped nail:

'Have they known and studied men who stop at nothing, men with boiling passions so unlike their own mild preferences for tea over coffee, or bridge over chess; men who have combined intelligence with utter ruthlessness, who were at once men of genius and without bowels . . . '

Before Neville could comment Woodhouse began to apologize: 'You find that a bit strong I suspect? I pulled – that impression from the air perhaps? Does it seem to you – er, a bit strong? Possibly a case – of sour grapes? You'll know he was – a kind of war hero? I was ploughed for the Army myself. Blind as a bat d'you see . . . '

Duff Gordon had been ruthless. When Neville had come round on the floor of the cottage in Vierzon to see that Curly's body and that of the German lieutenant had vanished, he had asked where they were. 'In the old duck-pond, legs tied to an iron wheelbarrow. They won't be coming to the surface in a hurry so don't worry. And if they should smell a bit, well, the pond's stagnant . . . ' Neville had noticed that Duff had retained the German's watch, and made some comment.

Duff's reply had been a jibe about 'a stinking tub of guts'. Neville had often thought that in maturity he would be far more critical of Duff's behaviour than he had been as a callow youth. But he was not going to join in an attack on the dead man.

Woodhouse sensed this and went on: 'Tell me – how much do you know about – tax evasion?' He gave a brief, formal laugh. 'Believe me – this is not an attempt – to compromise you.'

'Not all that much. I run a small business. I've known one or two people who have come a cropper over tax. I've never been anxious to emulate them. Do you mean keeping two sets of books – one for yourself and one for the accountants – that kind of thing?'

'Very much so. Duff Gordon had a rather – I'm speaking with more latitude – than someone in my profession usually allows himself – a rather, er, poor accountant. A one man band – out in rural Essex – Colchester, in fact. A bad thing to economize on. Best is cheapest you know. Perhaps at the time – it seemed a good idea. For years this – accountant, er, prepared a profit and loss sheet – duly signed the account – and the tax men did not object. But last year Duff Gordon came to me – with a problem. It appeared that doubts had arisen – there was some question of a back duty investigation. Do you know what that involves? All papers for the previous fifteen years – to be produced – then put through an exhaustive investigation – by their human computers. I gave Duff the best advice – you know they can sue you for treble tax? – I could on the spur of the moment. But he did not come back – so, naturally, I presumed that – the trouble had passed over. Now it seems – there is still some doubt . . . Personally I think it unlikely – the tax people will move against Karin – Mrs Gordon – but we shall see. As things stand – she is not at all – er, well off. Even when the house is sold . . . ' Woodhouse seemed to have lost track of his original line of thought. His sentences became even more laboured before petering out.

He picked up the bulkiest folder and slapped it down on

the desk. 'The technicalities – the legalities are endless. Tell me – you really haven't any idea – how you are to collect the money? Give me your thoughts.'

Neville said quite openly: 'None at all. If Mrs Gordon, you and the accountant don't have any leads for me to follow, there is nothing I can do.'

Woodhouse nodded away in silence for a few moments as he brooded on this. 'I'll tell you the position – as I see it. Duff Gordon was essentially a gambler. He chose to do this – gambling – in various odd fields of business – rather than on the horses. What we have in these books are – minute records of income and expenditure – which somehow don't make sense. The only thing that is clear is that – his financial affairs were – gradually reaching a crisis. All in all, this is – the balance-sheet of a man – ready for death – a candidate for suicide . . .'

'Do you mean that may have been what happened? That he drowned himself?'

Woodhouse employed his automatic false laugh again. 'Oh no! Firstly, I should not think of – committing myself – on that. And indeed – knowing Duff – it seems improbable. But to anyone who can read – a balance-sheet – his position was clear. He badly needed money. The bank was pressing him – to clear his overdraft. A compulsive gambler, Duff – and one whose luck had run out. Surely – if there was some business – that could be converted – quickly into cash – he would have done it himself. Perhaps his position changed – subsequently to writing to you.'

Woodhouse permitted himself his first gesture during the interview, an elegant wave of the hand as if dismissing something from his presence, and went on. 'It's rather a joke really. With regard to – probate – er, you probably know – we send an affidavit – to the Estate Duty Office. On the basis – of a first estimate – the executor pays duty – and is the owner of the estate. Then there is – a corrective affidavit. In all this – the principle involved is – *certum est quod certum reddit potest.* Roughly translated – that which can be found is certain – or can be treated – as being certain. Certain! Ha!' He flung the files back into an open drawer. 'With this estate – one feels like echoing Pilate – "What is truth?" '

Foolishly, impulsively, Neville had been on the point of telling Woodhouse that the timing of Gordon's letter made the suggestion that the debt had already been recovered most unlikely. But, as the man drawled wearily on, Neville had come to a decision to hold this back. For one thing, he had become certain that he was not going to get any useful information in Suffolk Street. Was he being treated to all this double-talk, a smokescreen of chatter, because Woodhouse really did not have it, or was reluctant to be in any way involved in something shady? More likely was the premise that Duff Gordon had kept his shady business with two partners as a secret both from his wife and his advisers. Neville was beginning to see that he had probably gone off on the wrong track in trying to follow up the deadhand letter himself: it was possible that it was only the first of a series planned by Duff Gordon to be delivered at intervals, which he had dictated and Barclays Bank was to put into effect.

6

'Mr Gabriel Brown, Packer's Mill, near Oxhey, Herts,' As Ralph Neville drove out of London for the second time in the humid heat of that July Wednesday, he had this address written on a piece of paper propped up before him.

Returning from Suffolk Street to his flat in Montagu Mews, he had heard his phone ringing and raced up the stairs hoping it might be Rachel. This was the day he was supposed to have phoned her at Walberswick and he had felt a pang of guilt about not doing this, but he had definitely lost the envelope bearing the sketch map and phone number. All he could remember about her aunt's cottage was its isolated position on the Squireshill Marshes. Lascivious thoughts about Rachel had teased him during the afternoon. He could imagine her mooning about the cottage naked except for her lime-green wrap. He found it difficult to put sensual images of her out of his head. At times she reminded him of Oscar Wilde's quip about 'a de luxe edition of a wicked French novel got up for the English market'.

He had been worried that the bell might stop ringing and snatched off the receiver, willing it to be her gaily greeting him 'Hello darling,' and arranging a meeting for the following day, but instead of her cheerful voice there had been the noise of a throat being cleared and some coughing, followed by an old man's wheezy tones: 'Is that Mr Neville, Mr Ralph Neville? Very well then. Mr Gabriel Brown speaking. I'm an old friend of Duff Gordon's. Have you been away? Tried your number half-a-dozen times yesterday. Three calls again this morning.' Some more coughing, then a word came over the line that had a magical ring to it. 'Fiat. Do you understand? Fiat – Duff said we should use it as a kind of password. That you would know a French name beginning with V as another.'

'Vierzon?'

'Yes, that's it. Fiat-Vierzon. Very good. I want to see you. Can you come here? This afternoon? So much the better. It is urgent. We live at Packer's Mill, on the River Colne, not far from Oxhey. If you're coming by car I'll get my daughter to wait tea for you . . .'

The melody of the song 'Perfidia' which Glenn Miller had played so often in the early 1940s was spinning round in Neville's head during the latter part of his drive. The words were trite but had a special significance for him now. 'The gods above /Look down on what/Romantic fools we mortals be . . .' 'I found the love of my life in someone else's arms . . .' It was at once ironical and just that he should be experiencing pangs of carking jealousy over his imaginings concerning Rachel and the mysterious Gerald, surname unknown.

Now he could see quite clearly that if he had married Rachel his life with her would most probably have conformed to the pattern he discerned in Duff Gordon's marriage with Karin. At first they would have known a lot of physical pleasure – that kind of woman was exciting because she was acting out her own strong sexual drive instead of reacting to her partner's. But after sexual passion had waned then dissatisfaction on both sides would have set in. There was no doubt that eventually he would have received the same treatment as Sydney Mansell. And yet, knowing all this as well as the true worth of his own wife, if it had been Rachel on the phone he might well have been speeding towards Suffolk at the present moment.

For some time he had suspected that his obsessive feelings towards Rachel were the outlet for a self-destructive trait in him. What was it that curious cynic at the party in Charles Street had said about 'the relief of losing your no-claim bonus . . . of finally touching bottom'? It was possible that some hidden part of his character longed for an upset – to be found with Rachel by Sydney Mansell, or for some other dramatic happening to change his life for good or bad.

He saw the sign saying 'Private Road – Packer's Mill only – Trespassers will be Prosecuted' and turned off on to a rough track. The river Colne ran in a valley some sixty feet below the main road. The track which he followed went only a short way to a double garage. He parked his car there and then looked down, noticing how the river divided and joined again so that Packer's Mill was situated on a kind of island. The main stream of the river was nearest to him, and one had to cross over by a white-painted wood bridge. It was the mill-stream that formed the other boundary of the island, and its course was obscured by some of the mill buildings.

As Neville went down the path he felt as if the years were falling away from him, and all his grown-up attitudes were being sloughed off like layers of grime. He was approaching a scene much like one that had played an important part in his childhood and he had a sensation of revisiting that far-off epoch. As a youngster he had spent much of his time playing in and around a river very similar to the Colne. He and his friends had been particularly fortunate in that the fields bordering their river had led on to the estate of a long-deserted mansion so that, when they had tired of swimming in the river or wading in it to search for crayfish, they had been able to climb in the giant rhododendron bushes or fish for carp and rudd and the goldfish hybrids which remained in the artificial lake.

He stood on the bridge looking first back along the river in the Oxhey direction where it flowed through a wood and then towards the mill house. It seemed to brim the banks, deep and dark. At the edge he could see minnows swimming above the sandy bottom, and water-boatmen propelling themselves like miniature skiffs among the reeds.

'Mr Neville? Okay? Good,' A female voice called out from the mill house and for a moment he saw someone waving from the front door and then vanish.

The mill house was probably early Victorian, surmounted by a delightful clock-tower and a fanciful cupola. He could see that bits and pieces had been added to it through the years without spoiling the overall impression. The dark red brick was largely covered by virginia creeper.

'Mr Neville – there you are! I spied your Alfa as you turned off the road, then you disappeared for a bit. My name's Pamela Morant.' She was a tall woman with a lovely complexion and brown curly hair, dressed in paint-spotted jeans and a denim shirt. She had the vague and rather distracted look that he had often encountered in wives who had a lot of children and an insufficient income. She smiled, showing perfect teeth: 'It's my Dad who wants to see you. Do you think you could make your own way? To the end of the garden at the other side of the house. You really can't get lost. I don't want to appear rude but I'm jam-making and it's approaching a crisis. I'll be bringing tea shortly.'

Neville smiled back. 'I was lost for a few minutes – in admiration. This is my idea of a dream house and I must admit to plain envy. Which way do I go?'

'Through the passage at the end is best. That brings you out by the mill-race so please don't fall in. Then the path takes you straight to the spot where Dad will be. You probably noticed that this place looks like an island, roughly shaped like a ship. Well, Dad loves the bit of lawn near the prow.'

A Roman bust had been positioned on a ledge at the end of the house which Mrs Morant indicated: it looked back with a hint of proud derision at the dividing river and the wood through which the river flowed. Neville paused to touch the weather stone, finding pleasure in tactile contact with the noble face that had survived so many centuries and would probably be regarding the same unchanging view when all of Neville's problems were long forgotten.

He opened a half-glass door that led into a passage-way running the length of the house, used as a store-room for pieces of furniture and various oddments contained in cardboard cartons. He always experienced some strange fascination in the atmosphere of silent rooms and passages in houses existing for a long time unvisited. There was a dusty spotted mirror – the kind in which one might expect to spy ghosts. By the side of an out-moded wireless set he noticed the cobweb-covered wings and gleaming goblin eyes of a plump moth. The wall on his right hand side joined on to the main mill building and was spotted with damp-mould.

When he opened the twin door at the other end of the passage he stepped out beneath spreading branches of acacia and startled a blackbird which sped away with taunting cries of simulated panic. There were strong smells of meadow-sweet and newly mown grass, but the pervasive one was of river water.

A thick piece of rope had been fixed to an iron stanchion so that one could swing over or into the mill-race. Bright green moss looked like a rash on the pickled walnut colour of the oak piers.

Neville followed the path, pushing through an arcade of smothering greenery till it emerged on to a lawn by an ancient sundial incised with Jacobean moralizing. An old man dressed in a faded brown shirt and white trousers was asleep in a cane chair beneath a plum tree. There was a fat white dog by his feet, illustrating what went on in its dreams with aborted movements and faint whimpers. Mr Gabriel Brown's dangling fingers also fidgeted with something invisible.

Neville looked down on to the freckled bald head, not knowing whether to wake the old man, then walked on towards the end of the island, soon finding himself knee-deep in cow-parsley. The island was indeed shaped just like a ship, the prow being the point where the mill-stream joined with the river again. The ground there, covered with skunk cabbage, kingcup and royal fern, was treacherous but Neville made his way to a point only a few feet from where the last plants were suspended over water. The illusion of being on a boat was given a surrealistic twist by the current flowing away from the prow.

The sinuous, dimpling surface of the swollen river had a nearly mesmeric effect on Neville. He watched it absorbedly, thinking that his life was flowing away like that. With just such heedless pace minutes joined each other and were lost. How few of them he used to any purpose. It was a great stroke of irony that he had longed to find some cause or work more worth-while than dealing in 'bits and pieces', yet what had come to hand was a shady, possibly criminal affair.

He took his time retracing his steps. The heat which had been oppressive in London was tempered at Packer's Mill by a breeze blowing against the current of the river. He found a calm stretch of water, protected by a barrier of reeds, where he knew roach would be hovering. Then he stopped to enjoy the prospect of a rose-covered pergola and butterflies dancing over a lavender bed. All the time there was the background noise of the muffled roar of water going over the weir. In these idyllic surroundings ordinary business matters seemed nonsensical, let alone the intricacies of Duff Gordon's affairs.

When he returned to the shade of the plum tree Gabriel Brown was awake, mopping his face with a large yellow handkerchief, but he had to approach within a few paces before the old man gave any sign of acknowledging his presence: 'Someone there? Is that you, er, Mr Neville is it?'

'Yes, Mr Brown, sorry about disturbing you. And I'm sorry too that you had so much trouble in contacting me, but I've been out a lot the last two days.'

'Very glad you came. I'm an old friend of Duff's. Like you – I understand. Give me your hand. Duff trusted me.'

When they shook hands Gabriel Brown continued to stare hard at Neville's face with watering eyes, then he shook his head. 'No good. Hopeless. My eyes . . . You look just like a ghost, a snowman rather. Nothing dramatic about my eyes. Not cataract. A slow deterioration of the retina. Linked with anno domini and therefore quite irreversible. Everything looks as if it was made of cotton-wool. Tea here suit you?'

'Yes, thanks. I've been wandering around thinking how beautiful this place is. London's unbearably hot and crowded today – it seems like Bedlam compared with this . . .'

'That's fine then. My daughter will bring the tray to the end of the path and whistle. She's rather busy at the minute, making strawberry jam. You know, there's quite a business about the bottling . . .' The old man coughed and put his handkerchief to his mouth, but moisture left a streak on the brown-dotted back of his hand like a snail's trail. There were smoky pale circles round the irises of his eyes.

'That Duff! . . . ' The old man coughed and laughed at the same time. Then his lips moved a little before he started to speak again, like a moving picture just out of synchronization with the sound. 'There's no one like him! Quite unique. Veritable magician too. This business for instance. He said he had someone in mind – if – it was necessary. And by Jove! – here you are. Not my business – directly I mean. You understand that. But Duff talked to me a lot . . . My son-in-law Eugene Morant was one of Duff's two partners. Gene's a clever chap, but very nervous too. Always on edge, like a cat. He wanted me to sound you out first, see what I thought about you handling this affair. Of course, really I don't know half of what goes on . . . ' He bent down to stroke the still sleeping dog's back. 'Like Toby here, I've lived too long. Still, Gene seems to trust my judgement . . . '

Neville heard a whistle and stood up. 'That will be the tea. I'll fetch the tray.'

Gabriel Brown got up too. 'I'll come with you. Stretch my legs.' He held on to Neville's arm and began to walk with agonizingly slow steps.

'Are you like Duff? You're strong like him. Is that why he asked you? Are you like him?'

'Not really. I'm rather persistent though, and he knows I stick at things. He told me in a letter that he needed someone who wouldn't take no for an answer.'

They made slow progress in a thoughtful silence till they came to the tea-tray which was set with plates of sandwiches, brown bread-and-butter and a jar of honey.

On the way back to their chairs the old man began a ruminative monologue: 'Cucumber sandwiches. She'll have given us cucumber. Very refreshing on a day like this. Duff and Eugene – there's a third partner in the business. Jack Loring. I expect you'll meet him in due course. Great big chap. Had a stroke last year I understand. Otherwise he would have dealt with it no doubt. Duff dying like that and Jack having a stroke – it's all made Gene that much nervier.

Duff used to bring his girl – Liz – with him when he came here. He livened things up, believe me. He put up that rope for swinging across the mill-race. And he'd take the kids over the weir on one of those lilos. What a fellow he was! He used to make me think of those lines by Browning:

> You see one lad o'erstride a chimney-stack;
> Him you must watch – he's sure to fall, yet stands!
> Our interest's on the dangerous edge of things.'

Neville helped Gabriel Brown to a sandwich and poured out some tea. The old man took a big swig of tea, then ruminated again. 'Funny about death. When you get to be my age, of course, you're always hearing that so and so's fallen off his perch. Only the other day, read in the *Daily Telegraph* of the cremation of a great chum of mine, known him since I was five . . .'

Gabriel Brown stopped talking and pushed a piece of sandwich round his plate. It was apparent that he was mentally pursuing the consequences of the newspaper announcement. Neville thought how the old man must be preparing, even if only in the darkest recesses of his mind, for his own final journey. He avoided looking at him, fearing some facial nakedness should betray the old man's private thoughts.

'But Duff. What age was he? Fifty odd. And so strong, vital . . . Never known anyone like him for energy. Full of life – that's funny – saying that . . . But you haven't come here to hear an old man philosophize. I'll tell you something that's true, though, about old age. When you look back you feel as if you must have lived several lives – I simply can't connect the dodderer I am now with the chap I was at thirty . . .' He wet his fore-finger and dotted it over his plate to pick up sandwich crumbs, then said: 'Tell me. Have you been told anything about the business?' He lowered his voice, as Karin Gordon had done when Neville had been closeted with her in the small room. 'Has it got anything to do with gold?'

Neville found it difficult to keep a note of amusement out of his voice as he said: 'But I know nothing about it. I'm just waiting to be told something myself.' He remembered the photograph of the nondescript man and the Job quotation 'I shall come forth as gold' but he was not inclined to take that literally.

The old man ignored this outburst, going through a half-hearted performance, like a remembered pattern of behaviour which could not be dropped, of looking to see if they might be overheard. 'The whole business – very hush-hush of course. You'll know that. But I once heard the three of them talking here. Last year it was. And Duff said quite distinctly "There'll be much gold". His exact words. Can hear him now.'

'I see . . . ' Neville could not help shrugging, though he knew the old man's sight would not take in this disclaimer: 'I don't think that means much. It's a slang term now, just signifies a lot of money – not necessarily gold. I must say I'm impatient to find out more myself. How I'm supposed to help and so on. I want to do what I can but . . . it's rather frustrating. I expect your son-in-law will put me in the picture.'

'Of course. I shall tell him to depend on you, Neville – I want to drop the Mister if I may. He'll be glad to have someone he can rely on to help. I know he's been worried. He's away just at present but I'll get him to contact you as soon as possible. Ah, did you hear that call? My daughter – wanting to know if we need a fill-up for the tea-pot. Will you go?'

The errand for hot water involved admiring some rows of jars filled with strawberry jam, and took longer than Neville anticipated. When he returned Gabriel Brown had fallen asleep again and was snoring quietly. It was a tranquil sound that chimed in well with the noise of the wind in the reeds and the river flowing over the weir.

7

The morning after his enjoyable interview with Mr Gabriel Brown, Neville spent three hours in his shop in St Christopher's Place. Business had been good during his absence and he commented to Alida Patterson: 'Now I know the simple secret of making more sales – taking more holidays,' and told her that he was going to have two or three days by the sea but hadn't decided quite where. There was some kind of sneaking pleasure in the mere contrivances of adultery: it was a lonely, often a sad business, but he would have to confess to enjoying both the complicated arrangements and the time spent in anticipating the next meeting.

He glanced through his mail quickly before opening any letters in case there might be another registered communication from Barclays Bank. A feeling of anti-climax at not finding one was dissipated on seeing a parcel which he thought was addressed in Rachel's hand. Like a love-sick youth, he was impatient to see both what it enclosed and whether she had sent a note in the parcel. She had only written to him once before, a brief letter shortly after they had met: 'How glad I am that we came together in the strange way that lovers do.' He had hidden this letter in a cardboard box under some sheets of used carbon paper. He had imagined that this simple subterfuge would keep it safe from other eyes, but his experience in going round Duff's study had driven home the necessity for destroying the sole documentary evidence of his illicit relationship.

Immediately Alida Patterson left the shop to have coffee he ripped off the brown paper and corrugated card to find a handsome edition of *Anna Karenina* bound in black morocco. The binding was so subdued, indeed sombre, yet elegant that he half suspected the source of the gift. This was confirmed when a sheet of thin azure paper slipped out of the book and drifted to the ground.

Dear Ralph,

A consolation prize for a gallant loser. Please let us hear from you soon or Dan's sense of guilt over your encounter with the madman during that blessed clue-hunt (we've given them up forever!) may become inoperable. We hardly move from the phone in case you should ring. Ruby has been trying to find you: she says she used to have a nightmare in which she was made Mayor of Calcutta; this has now been replaced by one in which she comes to your shop and finds it has vanished! So please write or phone.

Yours as ever

Mary

Neville sat down and wrote notes to the Priests and Ruby Abrams. When Alida Patterson returned he went out for some coffee himself, taking a road-map to plan his trip to Southwold. Sitting in the café, he overheard two other antique dealers talking about the possibility of making a million pounds or at least the price of a lunch from some deal. The conversation interested him when it was concerned with porcelain jars in the Kutani and Kakiemon styles, then irritated him when it settled down to endless bragging about bargains found in bygone days, peppered with weighty sentiments such as 'There's nothing like getting a few bob to cure socialism'. He found it impossible to concentrate on the map and finished his coffee quickly.

When he returned to his shop, Alida Patterson was holding the phone. She waved to him and said: 'Good. I hoped you might come back in time. A Mr Morant – on some private matter.' She handed him the receiver and went into the small back room.

'Ralph Neville here. Is that Mr Eugene Morant?'

A light boyish voice replied: Yes. Look, I'd very much like to see you this morning if poss. It was good of you to travel out yesterday to the Mill to meet the old boy, but I shall only take up a few minutes of your time. I'm at Baker Street station now.'

'Fine. Would you like to come to my shop? Just off Wigmore Street. Or my flat in Montagu Mews?'

'Don't like to sound odd but I'd prefer – some neutral ground. I'll explain why when we meet.'

Neville thought this sounded extremely odd but said: 'Okay. Name your spot.'

'Fine. Look, old lad, do you have your passport handy? I mean, could you put your hands on it before we meet?'

Neville pondered this question for a moment though he knew the answer. 'Yes, my passport's in the drawer of the desk where I'm sitting at the moment. Why? I hope I shan't need it to meet you. Where is this neutral ground?'

Morant gave a nervous laugh that was supposed to be reassuring: 'No – I just think it would be a good idea for us both to produce our passports so that we can have a quick dekko and be absolutely sure who we are talking to. I know this sounds mad but humour me, eh?'

'Right. I'll bring my passport. Where?'

'St Katharine's Precinct. Do you know it? Anyway you can't miss it. On the east side of Regent's Park. Just north of Cumberland Terrace. A quirky bit of Gothic-cum-Tudor architecture in mellow brick. You'll find that just to the right of the sign pointing to the Pastor's House at the Danish Church there's a replica of a runic stone. We can have our little confab there. Can you make it in half-an-hour?'

'Easy. See you.'

Neville frowned as he replaced the telephone and took out his passport. Chosen by a dead man, vetted by a blind man, and now he was to be briefed by a nut who preferred to conduct conversations by a runic stone. But any irritation at Morant's eccentric request had disappeared by the time Neville drove away from Montagu Mews. There on the back seat of his Alfa Romeo Duetto lay the suit-case packed for his trip to Suffolk, and he had promised himself that whatever complications ensued from the meeting with Morant, the day would certainly end with the Alfa being parked in Southwold.

There were some moments of pleasure to be experienced in

the drive round Regent's Park. He enjoyed the sight of Decimus Burton's stucco villa 'The Holme'. Just glimpsed through the trees, it appeared like a piece of dream architecture. And it was a perfect summer day with a breeze that would ward off any humidity. Above all Neville enjoyed feeling fit again and being in a rather bouncy mood: he was ready to deal with anything that Morant had in store for him.

After parking his car in the Outer Circle Neville took a minute to glance through the triumphal arch at the inspired perspective of Chester Terrace, then he walked slowly along the length of Cumberland Terrace strung out so grandiloquently with porticoes all round and the delightful Coade stone figures on the pediment. There was no one waiting in the precinct of the church. Neville walked up to a notice, THE PASTOR'S HOUSE – TIL PRAESTE-BOLIGEN, then saw a large stone decorated with primitive designs to his right. He had just begun to read about 'The Jelling Stone' when he heard light footsteps and swung round. He felt inclined to act nearly as cagily as Eugene Morant.

A slim man was approaching with a rather hesitant step as if being twitched along by an invisible puppeteer. He waved a passport like a white flag. 'Hallo there, Neville. Sorry about all this cloak and dagger stuff. But I'm acting under orders. I was told to approach you strictly on the q.t. you see.' His manner was nervous and humbly apologetic. He handed his passport to Neville, who did the same.

Eugene Robert Morant's passport had been issued only four years previously but there was some sign of ageing even in that period, to judge from the photograph. Nervousness was acting like some kind of subtle decay in him. According to the particulars he was fifty years old, five feet ten inches in height, with grey hair. His occupation was discreetly listed as 'Company Director'. Neville flicked through the pages negligently, saying, 'Very good. I'm quite convinced you are none other than the veritable Eugene Robert Morant.'

Morant winced. 'I can understand you feeling a little irritated by all this hush-hush business – must seem absurd to you – but I'm only taking pains to do things right this time.'

His hazel-coloured eyes were troubled. His manner was flawed by a lack of confidence: he acted like someone engaged in selling a worthless object. 'Thing is you see I had this odd letter which Duff had arranged for his bank to send on to me. And, as Duff would have put it, I went off at half cock. Contacted his wife – Karin. Now I am reliably informed I screwed things up a bit by doing so . . . '

'I did the same,' Neville broke in. 'I went to see her too. It seemed a natural enough thing to do.'

'Yes, perhaps, for you. I understand you haven't been in touch with them for years. But I knew there was a state of domestic tension in that house – lots of awful flare-ups. I might have known that Duff kept this business to himself.'

'Who told you it was a mistake to go to Mrs Gordon?'

Morant's eyes shot round nervously as if this sudden question might prompt him to make another mistake. He stuttered another apology: 'S-sorry, old lad. M-my lips are sealed on that point.' He took out a large red snuff-taker's handkerchief and touched his nose with it. The action seemed to be a formality to give him time to calm down and think. 'The position is that Duff has left us dummy hands to play. If we do just that, play the cards exactly as he wanted, then everything should go off as planned.'

'One question I should like answered,' Neville commented. 'I'm a little puzzled why if you were Duff's partner you can't wind up the business yourself.'

'Good question.' Morant passed the handkerchief across his face with a hand that was visibly trembling, so that his answer became rather superfluous. 'Firstly, I have a weakling's talent for imaginative dramatization. Secondly, in business I have all the impact of a conjurer who's left his white rabbit on the bus. It's true Jack Loring and I were nominally Duff's partners, that is to say we had a financial interest, but it was always Duff who managed everything. It could only be kept going for so long by someone with his talent for tight-rope walking.'

Neville said: 'Seeing Duff's study with all those maps and the transceiver, knowing that he owned various boats, made me wonder if the "business" had something to do with smuggling. Gold for instance?'

'Good Lord no – nothing like that.' Morant's denial was so spontaneous and vigorous that it carried conviction, much more so than anything else he had said. 'His boats were a hobby, practically a passion with him. Personal. Nothing to do with the business . . . ' He faltered a bit and when he continued the rest of his statement sounded a little disingenuous: 'The business is just a kind of confidence trick, a trick of confidence rather. The point is that it needed someone like Duff to do it. The funny thing is that we decided last year, after Duff had the heart trouble, to wind it up this year anyway. Trade in the contract for a cash settlement.'

'But, according to the cards Duff has left you to play, you can't tell me anything definite about the business?'

'Nothing positive. I can tell you it's not smuggling, it's not robbery, negative stuff like that. And you can always drop out you know. But Duff seemed to think you would pull it off for us. He must have thought you had the talent for the job – the nerve.'

Morant's last sentence hovered between being a compliment and a subtle insult. Neville shrugged and said: 'I knocked Duff out once. In a boxing championship. It may have given him a lopsided view of my potentialities. But I'm not backing out. I'll give it a go. Tell me what I have to do.'

Morant took an envelope from an inside pocket and opened it to extract a printed form. Neville could see that it was headed 'MIDAS SECURITY COMPANY, The Minories, London, E.C.3'. Morant wrote his name at the bottom of the form.

'My brief ends with signing this docket and giving it to you. You take it to Jack Loring and get his signature, then I suppose he will add his bit of the jigsaw. Jack lives in the same place where Duff used to hang out, Burnham, in Essex. This is his address.' He wrote 'Jack Loring, Wick Farm, Burnham-on-Crouch, Essex' on the envelope, sealed it and handed it to Neville.

Neville looked at it thoughtfully. 'I want to go to Suffolk

today, but I suppose I could call in at Burnham on the way?'

'Nothing easier. Hardly off your route. You'd take the A12 anyway I expect. Well, you just turn off at Chelmsford for Burnham, then get back on it for Colchester and Ipswich, Suffolk in general.'

'Shall I be able to find it easily? I mean the farm. Any directions?'

'You'll have to park your car in Burnham. There's only a bumpy track out to the Wick Farm area, not suitable for cars. Matter of walking, or I expect Monica Loring would get someone to meet you in a jeep if you don't fancy walking two or three miles.'

'No. I'll walk. Perfect day for it.'

Morant relaxed visibly and rubbed his hands. 'That's it then. You'll pull it off I know.'

Neville shrugged. 'It's a case of suck it and see.' He shook hands with Morant, pocketed the envelope addressed to Loring, and walked off.

When he had nearly reached the road, Morant shouted out: 'But you'll be careful, won't you? That's important. Is that clear?'

Neville called back: 'Crystal.'

8

'Each man is driven irresistibly by his passion.' The one line of Virgil that had stayed in Neville's memory since his schooldays was another example of prophetic retention, for at fifteen it could have meant little to him. Thirty years later he was indeed driven by his own passion, a hunger for those moments he had sometimes found in love-making, fleeting seconds when an equipoise or harmony with some kind of secret life could be achieved, when for an instant the world seemed to be ideally organized after all.

The knowledge that his next rendezvous with Rachel was only a few hours away made the side-tracking journey to Essex seem to pass quite quickly, though it took more than an hour to drive through the concrete jungle that stretched from Whitechapel to Romford.

The countryside after the Chelmsford by-pass was flat and uninteresting, and made to appear even duller by the sky clouding over, but the very fact that he had turned off the road which led to Suffolk had a pleasurable aspect in its temporary delaying of the sensual delights to be found at his journey's end; very soon he would be passing the same signposts, lanes and fields, returning towards Walberswick and the cottage in the Squireshill Marshes accommodatingly vacated by Rachel's aunt.

It was nearly three p.m. when Neville drove into Burnham-on-Crouch and parked in the High Street. Through a gap between some houses he could see the grey water of the estuary indivisibly joined to the cloudy sky. The small town was covered with a drizzling mist, and a cool wind blowing in from the direction of the open sea made the humid heat of the previous day seem quite unreal. He walked through an alley-way on to the quay to discover more yachts than he had even seen in one place before. There was a pleasant-looking old pub called The Galleon. A festive noise came from the saloon bar, and when he opened the door he found the place was crammed with people nearly all of whom were talking and acting as if they had reached the end of a long drinking session. Apart from two quiet old men in battered navy-blue serge suits, who looked as if they might be sailors, it was a smartly dressed nautical crowd in blazers, white roll-necked pullovers, immaculate jeans and denim jackets. One man was dramatically rigged out in yellow oilskins. Neville was hungry as well as in need of a drink, and quite determined to get to the bar before closing time, but he enjoyed making slow progress through the crowd because of the patch-work quilt of conversation:

'Even when I'm out of control I'm still in control if you know what I mean.'

'Jolly boatin' weather I must say.'

'Roger said it followed him over from Le Havre.'

'From Le Havre? Roger? Well, if you can believe that you can believe anything. Le Havre? Southend more like . . . '

'Despite his hanging-judge mask and judicial manner you would have us believe that Roger lies?'

'In his teeth.'

The chatter made a pleasing counterpoint to Neville's private thoughts of Rachel's white arms and how she would appear when she unpinned her long black hair to let it fall about her shoulders. He was remembering her toasts when they were alone: 'Let the good things happen' and '*Vivre pour vivre*'.

He wanted to hear more about the lying Roger but a gap enabled him to move forward within reach of the bar, and he heard a solemnly drunk man in an immaculate black blazer and white trousers having difficulty in saying, 'No postmortem I promise you but . . . ' A plump, brassy blonde standing next to him was also dressed in yachting costume but on her it had a purely musical comedy effect. She looked glassy-eyed in Neville's direction and appeared appalled that he had nothing to drink: 'Whash the matter, dear, won't they give you no attention? Freddy! Freddy, this poor man, he's just longing for little drinks.'

Neville found himself wedged between the friendly woman and a small man helping himself greedily to shrimps, saying: 'Now you know what they say, your whelks is good for your night life, your oysters is highly amorous, your lobsters is lecherous, but your shrimps? Your shrimps is unbelievable.'

There was no sign that the pub was about to close: all the customers appeared reluctant to forsake its jolly atmosphere for their yachts at anchor in the mist. It was so noisy that it was essential to shout in order to be heard. Neville did so to order a pint of bitter. 'And do you have any sandwiches? A couple in a bag if you could? I'm going to walk to Wick Farm. Do you know the place? Belongs to Jack Loring.'

The relatively sober man taking Neville's order nodded at the end of each question. He pulled the pint of beer, then said, 'Very good beef. Prime Scotch wing rib. Wick Farm's quite a walk you know. You go out on the Quay and take the path along the river past the Yacht Club. Stick on it for about two miles and you'll see the Loring place. Not a farmhouse but a newish bungalow. Just watch out for a blotch of bright pink. Surrounded by a barn and other outbuildings. And a high wire fence. You should see it quite a way off.'

The man dressed in yellow oilskins was narrating some incident with histrionic gestures and Neville suspected that 'Roger' was substantiating his adventurous trip from Le Havre. This pub would have been Duff Gordon's local when he lived in Burnham, and Neville could easily imagine him in this convivial, nautical atmosphere. On the wall at the end of the bar there was a chart headed 'Der Tag' which showed the disposition of 'the British and German Fleets in Scapa Flow on the 21st November 1918 when the German Fleet surrendered', and other naval relics. An old ship's bell hung from the beams. Duff had been a Cockney though he had a remote Scottish ancestry, and he would have been very much at home in The Galleon among so many other Londoners who shared his enthusiasm for yachting. He would have recounted daring tales of sailing in forbidden waters without encountering any scepticism, then played the piano or sung songs like 'H'I'm 'Enery the h'eighth h'I h'am'.

It was three-fifteen and the crowd had begun to thin. Neville finished his pint and pocketed his sandwiches. Going out he heard Roger's critic saying, ' . . . he's gone over the edge, kind of thing. Lost touch with reality . . . '

On the wet cobbled quay small groups of people were standing about debating whether it was worthwhile doing any sailing in such miserable conditions, periodically staring at the horizon where the sun fitfully laid silver streaks on the grey sea.

Neville realized that it was unreliable weather which largely kept all pastimes in Britain at a pleasantly amateurish level: most sporting events were liable to be cancelled at short notice. It was indeed hard for any kind of fanaticism to thrive in a country where all flags were apt to go limp with rain and parades were often abandoned. He liked belonging to a nation of people who were good-humoured when disappointed. He walked slowly past a row of houses, noting names like 'Hove-to', 'Harbour-rest' and 'Sea Shanty', that fronted the river Crouch. There was a boutique for yachting clothes from the windows of which 'beautiful people' wax models stared out with haughty expressions.

After he had passed the Royal Burnham Yacht Club and the last straggling line of bungalows, Neville paused to eat his sandwiches. He surveyed the desolate area before him with pleasure that was heightened by the smell of sea-wind, the gulls' melancholy cries and the sound of curlews calling across the misty fields. A large bird which he did not recognize suddenly flew out of the mist, making a panicky warning call as though blowing through a comb and tissue-paper.

The slowly rising path was now bordered by sea-couch and marram grass. The mixture of sea and river water was a milky brown-grey colour, and the blocks of stone reinforcing the embankment were covered with sea-weed and the yellow froth of foam. He could see the rotting hulks of two schooners and the rusty remains of an ugly iron boat lined with four square tanks on each side. The land on his left was planted with barley and wheat, with an occasional intervening field of mustard, and bordering strips of dark green to show the site of dykes. Close at hand there was a notice in red: PRIVATE SHOOTING. The horizon was now lost behind a veil of mist.

He took out his map which was not so detailed as the chart in Duff Gordon's study, but it showed that the path would eventually lead him to the Dengie Flats. The Foulness and Maplin Sands area where Duff had been drowned was to the south of where he was standing, joining on to the other side of the estuary. Wick Farm was not marked on his map, but he found a place called West Wick near to Twizzlefoot Bridge.

He walked for half-an-hour before he saw a small oblong pink building, surrounded by islands of mist. There did not appear to be a path leading to it from the one that he was taking, so he ran down the steep embankment on his left and skirted a field of barley. Mist was now blowing in steadily as if to demonstrate what Liz Gordon had told him about this area. Through its hazy barrier he spotted a black car parked across another field, so it appeared that local farm-workers must know some way of reaching it through the lanes from the minor road which ran to the north over Muscle Bridge.

The islands of mist were joining up to form a sea flowing round him but there was no doubt that he had found the right place. The bungalow covered with pink pebble-dash was just as the barman had described it, built beside a ramshackle weather-boarding barn quite out of plumb. It was a shoddy building which looked as if it might have been designed on the back of a cigarette packet. Half a boat had been tacked on to it to form an eccentric kind of porch. The reason for the high wire fence became apparent once he was within a hundred yards of the place and heard ferocious barking. Two black alsatians were repeatedly throwing themselves up against the barrier as if in competition to see who could break out first.

A large blonde woman dressed in a pink blouse, white cardigan and royal-blue trousers appeared in the boat-porch. She said something quietly that transformed the guard dogs into pets who meekly trotted out of sight. The gate in the wire fence was of the kind more usually encountered on entering a tennis court, held in place by a flat iron bolt. Neville put his hand on it tentatively and called out: 'Mrs Loring? May I come in? I'm Ralph Neville. Did Mr Morant phone you?'

'Yes, of course, come in. Come in. I'm Monica Loring.' The large woman walked a little way down the cobbled path, smiling and shaking her head at some secret joke. 'Did the boys scare you? I expect they did. The tinkers! Jack's having a kip at the moment but he'll soon wake up. It's part of the business of the stroke you see, he suddenly nods off. One moment you're talking to him and the next he's away. Never mind, you can have a cup of coffee while we're waiting. You won't mind if I finish my snack? What with Jack being how he is, I have to pick at something when I can snatch a moment.'

Neville followed Monica Loring through a passage-way much encumbered by a laden out-size hallstand, numerous bulky coats and two large oil-paintings of sailing ships. The kitchen was as cluttered and untidy as Karin Gordon's rooms had been neurotically neat. Every flat surface was covered with pots, jars, papers and various oddments. Monica Loring poured some coffee essence into two cups and filled them with boiling water, then sat down with a sigh. 'Now – can I tempt you to join me?' She indicated a carton of ice-cream that lay on the table with the remains of a pork-pie, two jars of pickles and a bowl containing some mashed potato.

Neville shook his head. 'No thanks. I've had lunch but I shall enjoy the coffee.'

Monica Loring had the continual satisfied smile of a nun or a new convert. She opened the carton of ice-cream and put most of it on a plate, smothered it with chocolate flakes, then sat back and viewed the mixture with considerable satisfaction. She was about fifty, with hair that was as blatantly false in colour as the brassy blonde in the pub, but she had chosen to be a pink blonde and had achieved the effect of candy floss.

Neville pointed out the low window at the giant balls of

mist being blown around the barn. 'I suppose it was weather like this when Duff Gordon's boat was wrecked?'

'Very much so.' Monica Loring stopped smiling and a personality of more depth was revealed. 'The wind's blowing from the east now, as it did then. But later on it swung round to the north-east, and then was there a storm! Force ten winds. A terrific sea. The forecast was bad of course before he set off. But I expect you know Duff well enough to know he couldn't be told. He always did just what he wanted. Did you know he had some heart trouble? Last year it was when he told us, a hot June day in the garden here, and he was tucking into some strawberries and cream with me at the time. He heaped on the cream. So I said you're not worried about this cholesterol business then? And he said why worry, I'll take a chance, 'sides I'm told you meet a better class of person in Heaven. What a lad!' She began to eat the ice-cream with a dessert spoon but the large mouthfuls did not stop her talking rather breathlessly: 'You didn't go to the funeral, did you? It was a cremation at that miserable old Golders Green place. Karin didn't put an announcement in the paper. And there was no little meal or get-together after, nothing really. You can bet that hard piece Karin won't be putting in one of those nice In Memoriams either. I like them, don't you? There was a lovely one this morning. Listen to this.' She picked up a paper from the floor and read:

God saw that he was weary
And so He gave him rest
His garden must be lovely
For He only takes the best.

Neville had to struggle to suppress a burst of laughter that suddenly welled up: he bit the inside of his cheek, putting the desire to laugh out of his mind by thinking of the cold facts of Duff's death. It was an extraordinary business to imagine – the eventual overcoming of a man as strong and resourceful as Duff by the implacable sea.

Monica Loring pushed her plate to the other side of the table as if to fight the impulse to have a second helping. She shook her head to dispel the sentiment of the newspaper poem, and the matter-of-fact personality reappeared: 'You've got a docket for Jack to sign I believe. Eugene . . . ' She paused to frame her verdict on Morant: 'Poor Eugene, a bag of nerves he is now. Gone downhill, a write-off as far as the business is concerned. Lucky for him he's so good with his hands. Buys old properties you know, then gets them put into shape. The Morant Development Company . . . ' She shook her head again.

'I thought it was strange that he, Duff and your husband all chose to live by rivers. Is it just a coincidence?' Neville asked.

'Yes, really. Eugene doesn't like yachting or anything like that. He just fancied the mill house, bought it dirt cheap as it was derelict, and made it over. As for Jack, well, he was born at Paglesham, only a few miles from here. He's always been keen on the sea. Then in – 1950 I think it was – Duff came to stay with us for a holiday and he got keen on sailing too, so Jack kept his eyes open for a place for him in Burnham. Duff was happy here but Karin hated it, so eventually they moved to Chiswick.'

'This business that your husband shared in with Duff and Mr Morant – does it have anything to do with boats?'

Monica Loring looked cleverly at Neville: 'Ah, so you haven't been told what it is yet. No, nothing to do with boats. I can tell you that all you will be asked to do is to wind up the business. It's a kind of contract that can be sold for cash, but of course it has to be handled right. I can't say more as we had this letter that Duff arranged for his bank to send to us, and we intend to follow it word for word. I mean, we have to, don't we . . . '

Monica Loring broke off on hearing a muffled noise and left the room. Neville heard a muttered colloquy in which both 'the boys' and his own name were mentioned, and then she came back saying, 'Jack's awake now. He'll be able to sign that docket for you. The stroke only affected his left side.' They passed through a door, the top of which was of stained glass showing yachts with red, green and orange sails on a purple-blue background. The small living-room was as crowded as the kitchen, so that one was forced to edge a way round chairs. The walls were covered with paintings of sailing-ships. An unusually large man with a pasty face lay back in an arm-chair, a dachshund on his lap.

'Jack, this is the Mr Neville we've heard about. This is my husband, Mr Neville. He's not been well so he can't talk a lot.'

Jack Loring looked slack, as if all his muscles had been cut. He did not move in his chair when the introductions were made, but a faint smile gradually formed which twisted one side of his mouth downwards. He shook his head, so that it became apparent that he was about to say something: 'Ur, you, schlubble fine ish shplashe?' Monica Loring translated: 'He says did you have trouble finding this place?'

'Not really. I enjoyed the walk. I just stuck to the path on the embankment . . .'

Monica Loring broke in: 'Yes, and for God's sake do that on the way back. Don't try any short cuts or you'll land up in a dyke. Keep to that path and you can't go wrong.'

Neville handed over the envelope which Morant had addressed to Monica Loring, who produced a nail-file to open it with great care. When she took out the printed document she said to Neville: 'It's very valuable, this bit of paper; you'll stick to it tight won't you?' She held the page firmly in place while Jack Loring painstakingly added his signature at the bottom of the page.

'One more signature,' she said, 'and it's all stations go. So much bunce really. And frankly . . . ' She broke off to wave the paper about to dry the signature: 'We can just do with a little nest-egg. Jack used his contract money each year to plough into this place. But we sold off the farm when he had his trouble, and it didn't fetch a bomb. So a nice lump sum will be very welcome! I mean, we don't want to be dependent on our old-age pensions, do we?'

Jack Loring mouthed something, but Neville did not understand what he said. Monica Loring added soothingly: 'Yes, it's all going to work out. Depend on Duff to plan everything so we can go nap on it.' She got a roll of Sellotape out of a Toby jug with the idea of re-sealing the envelope, but the Sellotape began to demonstrate that it, like other inanimate objects, had a life of its own, sticking to her fingers, the arm of her chair and some nail-scissors. Jack Loring began to shake with suppressed amusement, saying something slurred about 'Seven, seven'. She translated again: 'He's laughing about old Duff hoping to meet the better class of person in Heaven.' She managed to seal the envelope after juggling ineptly for a minute, and handed it back.

'Righty-ho, there you are then. Everything should go like clockwork now. Well, we won't try to keep you. Eugene said you would be in a hurry to get off somewhere.'

Neville said good-bye to Jack Loring, who lay back in his chair with a sigh as if he had had enough of visitors for one afternoon. Monica Loring hummed a hymn as they went to the front door. 'I understand you knew Duff in the Army. Is that true?' She said this doubtfully.

'Yes.'

She shook her head. 'I don't know. You don't look quite old enough somehow to have been in it during the war.'

'I went in at seventeen, and it was towards the end of the war.'

'Really?' She stared at him as if this was very hard to credit, then shrugged. 'Oh well, I wish you luck, I wish us all luck.' Her tone was breezy. 'Look, don't go wandering round that barley field now the mist is so thick. Follow the hedge from our gate. It runs straight for about a hundred feet. There are two elder bushes at the end. From there you can see a short path up to the top of the embankment. Turn right once you're on it and Bob's your uncle.' She held out a workaday hand and gave Neville a nice smile. 'I trust you, and I feel sure you're going to bring back the bacon. But then it's like Duff to know the right one to trust . . .'

The mist was so thick that Neville could see barely twenty feet and he knew that if he had been twirled round, as in a game of blind man's buff, he would have completely lost his sense of direction; he was grateful that Monica Loring had pointed out the short cut to the embankment path. The curlews had stopped calling and the only noises were those of a fog-horn and some occasional dull thuds. Neville touched the much-sealed envelope in his pocket as he followed the hedge. The task of discovering some definite information about Duff's illicit business was so laborious that he felt he might possibly be involved in an elaborate hoax. Morant's extreme nervousness and Monica Loring's gratitude were against this, but still the word 'scapegoat' hovered in his mind as 'perfidious' had done when he was on the point of going to sleep in the hospital.

He walked round the second elder bush and came face to face with the man who had attacked him in the Turkish baths. The fat man stared at him with a scornful expression and said, 'So there you are,' with a note of malicious longing in his voice.

Neville experienced a mixture of excitement, amusement and exhilaration. To face up to a physical peril was for him to lose an inner tension, some psychological tyranny from the past. Moments of danger had always acted on him like this: the shock sharpened his reflexes, the sense of amusement gave him a feeling of detachment so that he watched the event while taking part in it. He rubbed his nose with his right hand and said, 'Clang. Seconds out. Second round,' but the fat man was not amused. The feeling of exhilarating release for Neville was compounded this time by a rare desire for vengeance. He had fought upwards of a hundred bouts in the boxing-ring from his schooldays onwards, but could not remember previously wanting to hurt anybody, to inflict real physical punishment. He thought: 'I'll make an exception in your case because of your smile when you nearly broke my back.'

He ran forward, lightly darting out a probing left to get the fun and games started. The fat man called out, 'Here! Ted!' and dodged the blow ponderously; he was muscle-bound and would do his best fighting in a telephone-booth. Somewhere in the mist a man's voice called out in irritation: 'For Christ's sake, Margolis! Where are you? Margolis!'

Margolis raised his thick neck with a movement like that of

a tortoise to call: 'Here, Ted. I've got . . . ' before Neville caught him with a right cross in the mouth. Margolis countered with a chopping blow that seared the edge of Neville's ear. With 'Ted' somewhere close, Neville knew that he had only a minute or two and must take a chance. He jabbed twice with his left, tried a right hook, weaving and ducking, then appeared to slip, going down on his left knee and bringing up a right upper-cut from the ground. Luck and a slow opponent were essential for the success of the blow, but when it came off the effect was dramatic. Margolis's jaw shut with a crunch and his eyes looked as if the light in them had been switched off. He tottered forward as though on artificial legs. Neville stepped back and hit the half-conscious man with a punishing left and right combination as though he was trying to fell a tree. Margolis went down, buckling at the knees, throwing out a fat hand that curled momentarily round Neville's wrist.

Neville heard footsteps behind the hedge and ran off, taking the steep slippery path up the embankment. He threw himself down in the sedge at the top and waited. A lithe man with crew-cut hair, in a black windcheater, appeared and bent down over Margolis's inert body, lifting up his head. Neville slowly wriggled backwards till he was out of the patch of sedge, then began to crawl along the path. After he had made this ignominious form of retreat for a few minutes, he got up and began to run through the wall of mist towards Burnham.

9

Headlong – a sensation of tumbling through space ended a mixed-up dream that had turned without warning into a nightmare. When Neville was jolted out of it by the impression of crashing into something unseen, the impact was vivid enough to induce him to raise his arm. He found on waking that there was a homely explanation for both sensations: his head had slipped down a few inches on the car seat, making him lie awkwardly, slumped with his legs pressed against the door and his arm now touching the window.

The drive from Burnham-on-Crouch to Suffolk had been a slow and tedious business; at first because of the thick mist which extended some twenty miles inland from the Thames estuary; after this had thinned he had been held up by heavy traffic on the main road which had come practically to a stand-still in Colchester. Finally there had been the frustrating delay of a punctured tyre. After changing the wheel Neville had stopped to have the spare repaired, and then decided to pull off the road for a few minutes' nap as he did not want to arrive at Rachel's doorstep feeling tired.

In his dream some of the experiences and sensations of the past few days had been cleverly blended into a passable imitation of a normal summer day at his country cottage: the dream garden had mysterious access to a river and he had been continuously aware of the muffled roar it made going over a weir; and Rachel had been installed as a member of the household, cheerfully accepted both by Helen and his children. Time had passed peacefully apart from a bizarre conversation with Duff Gordon in which Neville had been trying to justify his relationship with Rachel, gesturing uncharacteristically and gratuitously commenting on Gordon's own marriage. Apart from the pleasant sound of the river in the background, there had also been an intermittent thudding noise like that of distant thunder. Neville realized that his wily subconscious had in this way incorporated the sound of passing cars, like a cook who uses everything to hand. His strange conversation with Duff had been broken off when his son ran up to join them: that event had been like the wave of a magician's wand in a fairy story which changes everything. The garden had vanished and Neville had been thrown into black space through which he dropped with a profound feeling of emptiness and despair.

He glanced at his watch and saw with dismay that it was nearly twenty minutes to ten. Instead of a few minutes' nap, he had slept for over an hour. There was only a short drive remaining to Southwold, but by the time he had parked the car and walked to the Squireshill Marshes it would probably be ten thirty. He cursed himself for having stopped at all and drove on quickly, making the best time he could along a narrow winding road. Rachel had said something about a romantic, moonlight approach to her aunt's cottage and it looked as if he was going to have that experience. The sky had been flushed with an opal light in the west when he had driven off the road on to a grass verge, but now it was quite dark, largely obscured by rapidly moving nimbus clouds. The full moon, appearing fitfully from the ragged clouds, cast a dramatic light on the rather humdrum landscape of flat fields.

Once he had passed the signpost for Southwold Neville's sense of urgency relaxed a little, and he began again to think about the dilemma posed by Margolis. Knowing the fat man's name should make it a relatively simple matter for him to be traced by Detective-sergeant Rossiter, but Rossiter couldn't be given the name without mentioning other matters. It seemed probable that Margolis was linked in some way with the Duff Gordon affair but this was not certain: it was still possible that Sydney Mansell was behind Margolis. Both explanations had reasons against them: he could not really imagine Sydney Mansell instigating an attack by a thug; on the other hand the first attempt in the Turkish Baths had taken place before he had even opened Duff Gordon's letter, let alone made any attempt to follow up its mysterious message. After pursuing the problem for a few moments Neville decided to shelve it for at least twenty-four hours. Only Rachel knew his present destination, so Margolis could not appear in Suffolk. This makeshift attitude he knew was typical of his life. No doubt Sydney Mansell had already made plans for 1971 but Ralph Neville was concerned only with the immediate future. It was an attitude he felt he shared with Monica Loring and that probably explained his fellow-feeling for her. If he could wind up the curious Duff Gordon 'business', handing some of the cash over to the Lorings would be a considerable part of his reward.

Driving into Southwold was in a way like continuing his dream in that the charming small town appeared to be asleep or uninhabited. The dark windows, the deserted streets in which several houses were decorated with ships' figure-heads, the empty alley-ways and greens made a dream-like landscape, as did the sudden view of the moonlit beach and sea.

When Neville had parked his car he paused for a moment, wondering whether he should take his case. Tucked in between shirts, cradled in tissue-paper, there was a gift for Rachel, an eighteenth century enamel patch box decorated with two lovers standing against a pastoral scene encircled by the emblem THE GIFT IS SMALL BUT LOVE IS ALL. He hesitated about taking this and a carrier-bag containing two bottles of Château Grillet, then decided to leave such things till the morning as he liked the idea of arriving at the cottage carrying nothing, like a wayfarer who came knocking by chance.

As he began to walk across the common he paused again, looking back at the effect of moonlight on fences and roofs, knowing that this moment would become idealized for him, stored up among his nostalgic memories. The wind was blowing in directly across the North Sea, moaning between houses, but the desolate sound only heightened his anticipated pleasure. How fortunate he was to have an assignation with a woman as lovely and desirable as Rachel. His experience of inducing a headache for Susan Latymer had dispelled any lingering illusions about his attraction for women in general. He squirmed at the memory of his conversation with Susan in which he had used the encounter with the Hell's Angels youth to talk about his experience at Vierzon, ignoring the fact that the war must seem remote and unreal to her.

He tried to shake off the embarrassing memory by taking in details of the landscape, noting how it differed from the one through which he had walked in the afternoon. The Blyth estuary was much less bleak and flat than that of the river Crouch. On either side of the winding path he was taking the gorse grew quite high, and there were clumps of other bushes and the occasional tree. A young boy and girl were walking along the same path, about a hundred feet ahead, so he slowed his pace in order not to overtake them. Rachel had seemed quite anxious that his approach to her aunt's cottage should not be noticed.

In the night all smells and sounds were emphasized. The young lovers had paused to kiss and Neville stopped too. Then a moment later he heard them click-clacking across a Bailey bridge that straddled the river Blyth. When he came to the other side of the river he caught sight of the cottage tucked away in a hollow. The moonlight threw his deformed shadow, like that of Daddy Long-Legs, towards it. An owl shrieked and there was a piteous cry of some animal. The wind was flattening the reeds, forcing them this way and that. It was indeed a romantic approach to the Squireshill Marshes, as Rachel had prophesied: he burned to reach her, suddenly fearing that by some dream-like trick she would have vanished or changed. The strong wind was blowing all the clouds away and the next day would probably be fine. How wonderful it would be to wake in the cottage and see the dawn break, with the sun rising above the marshes and the sea.

The cottage was very small, washed white, with latticed windows and a thick reed thatch. There was no light to be seen, and Neville wondered if perhaps his journey was to be in vain after all, until he noticed that a bedroom window was open and the curtains were pulled downstairs which suggested that someone had spent the evening there. Two hedgehogs were snuffling about on the handkerchief-sized lawn. The garden borders were very small but full of flowers and the air was heavy with the scent of stocks. An over-size lavender bush grew by the misshapen front door. He knocked sharply, wondering what he could say if Rachel's plans had gone astray too and her aunt should still be in residence. Ten-thirty was not suspiciously late for a chance call and he could inquire if someone else lived there. He mentally rehearsed this but in his nervous state all the names that came to mind seemed bogus and improbable.

He knocked again, straining to detect the least sound. At the third knock he heard a muffled exclamation above and someone moving about there. After a few more minutes a light went on and the front door was opened an inch or two, and with great relief he saw it was Rachel in her green wrap, with her feet bare. He stepped closer to the gap to see that she had a strange expression – of fear or pain.

'It's me. All clear? Is it all right?'

'Oh Ralph!' She said this in an impassioned whisper but her look of apprehension did not change, and for a moment he thought she was not going to open the door wider.

'What's wrong? Something's wrong. Tell me.'

Rachel moved reluctantly backwards, letting her arms fall to her sides. 'God, why didn't you phone? You fool! – such a stupid trick coming like this! I told you to phone. Why didn't you?' Her voice was still hushed, but more tense than the situation seemed to dictate: it was as if she was getting keyed up for an approaching performance on an emotional tight-rope.

He took hold of her arms, hoping that physical contact and a few kisses would put things right as they had done with previous misunderstandings and quarrels. 'I'm terribly sorry darling. Really I am. But I lost that damned envelope and couldn't remember the Walberswick telephone number. All I could remember was my stupid joke about Candlestick 999. I had an accident, went to hospital, and the things were taken from my pockets.'

'But I phoned *you* – several times,' she said in the same quiet voice, ignoring the stuff about the hospital which he had hoped would dispel her annoyance. 'I phoned and phoned with no reply. So in the end I presumed you had been summoned by your better half and scurried off to Ireland.' She said this with tense gaiety, but he could tell there was more trouble to come. 'So I gave you up,' she added flatly.

'Well, I can only say I'm very sorry. I apologize, but you must see it was difficult for me. I couldn't very well send a telegram, not knowing your aunt's name – anyway I thought it might be compromising . . . ' He broke off making excuses and took her in his arms, but it was like embracing a reluctant stranger: her body was taut and she pulled away from him. Her eyelids fluttered like butterflies against his face. He tried to kiss her mouth but she turned away so that it touched her cheek. Her face was burning as if she was feverish. He could feel that she was wearing nothing under the thin wrap. Her heart pounded and her breasts moved against his chest, with the effect of an aphrodisiac, but he continued just to hold her gently, hoping that she would calm down. Over her shoulder he saw that there were two wine glasses and an empty bottle on the small table in front of the couch. In the corner of the room a record-player was still whirling silently with the head-piece bobbing up and down at the end of the record's groove.

It dawned on him that there was probably another reason for her distress apart from his bungling the rendezvous. 'Is your aunt here – is that it? Didn't she go after all?'

She hesitated for a moment as if unsure what to reply, then shrugged hopelessly, whispering: 'No, she's not here.' Her tone implied that his suggestion could not be more stupid.

'My God! – it's not Sydney?'

'No.' She gave an unhappy smile which he somehow found more disquieting than her other strange behaviour.

He pulled her round sharply so that he could look at her closely. There were tiny beads of sweat on her brow and her eye-black had run, leaving streaky lines as though she had been crying. She was trembling visibly. Her face had the pallor that he had seen on many occasions after they had made love. There was a tiny mark on her neck as if she had been bitten. When he looked into her eyes he knew what she could not tell him, but did not want to question her or believe her if she answered. He stood still, saying nothing, foolishly hoping that some miraculous trick would change everything, as seeing his son had changed his dream. She continued to smile, a faint unhappy smile in which guilt and fear were mingled. The touch of her breasts had stirred his sexual desire, but now this drained away and he felt cold, tired and empty. Sick too, as though he had been punched in the stomach.

At last he felt he must say something. He still held her shoulders, but his hands did not seem to make contact. 'Someone else? – there's somebody up there?'

'For Christ's sake . . . ' Before she could reply, this explosive outburst in a young voice came from the stairs and the next moment a dark-haired youth, bare-footed and dressed only in jeans, rushed across the room, giving Neville a hard push which caught him off-balance so that he nearly fell. 'I was wondering – when will the penny drop? I mean, how stupid can you get? Yes, you're right, there is someone else – so you're not wanted here. Push off.' The handsome dark-eyed youth followed this up by pushing again, with jerky nervous movements, striking Neville's face with his palm. The pain of this blow was out of all proportion to the force with which it was delivered, like some nightmarish punishment. The youth dropped his hands but repeated his warning: 'Go on – get out.' His tone was nervous and blustering, unsure of the true position and his authority.

'Stop it, Gerald!' Rachel said this sharply, but she added nothing to the command. Neville could not say anything: he stared at Rachel, waiting for her to decide his fate, while someone inside his head repeated over and over: 'The biter bit.' She seemed unable to comment on the unpleasant farce or to meet his eyes, and the three of them stood in silence – the only sound in the room being the wind whining in the chimney-piece. When she did look at Neville she had the false smile again, and a look implying that they had been playing a game, the rules of which she had always known but he had not.

Walking back along the short path, fumbling with the garden gate, he kept thinking that she would call out to him, but the detached commentator in his brain queried the point of this, pointing out that she could only offer him a night on the couch while she shared her aunt's bed with Gerald.

Now it was his turn to feel feverish and tremble, finding it difficult to keep on walking on numb legs. He passed over the Bailey bridge like an automaton, not caring which path he took on the other side of the river. An illusion which he had needed badly in his life had been whisked away, as a doctor's verdict might dispel false hopes, and now there was a basic impoverishment which he would have to learn to accept. Picking over his feelings was like sorting through a rubbish tip, discarding such trashy things as self-pity and wounded pride, searching hard for some residue, the love which he had believed they shared. Some perverse desire for self-punishment kept intervening, making him visualize the scenes in the cottage after he had left. No doubt Rachel would have been upset, probably giving way to tears; and Gerald would spend some time comforting her, holding her tight as she cried and through the aftermath of convulsive sobbing, and then . . .

Neville stopped walking and stared up at the clear moonlit sky, wanting to be rid of his sick imaginings. Othello's phrase, 'A cistern for foul toads to knot and gender in', came into his mind, though he knew how absurd it was; he had never considered his own love-making with Rachel to be toad-like. What he needed to do was to think firmly of how he had been willing to take the chance of inflicting a similar experience on Sydney Mansell, and the effects of jealousy on Helen. In the event he had received them instead – a swingeing blow. He said out loud, 'It couldn't happen to a nicer chap'; the ironic phrase summed up the situation.

Like a series of self-inflicted wounds, memories of times he had shared with Rachel came back to him: a whispered conversation in the small hours when words had lost their usual meaning, becoming exchanges in which the tone meant more than what was said, phrases changed to exclamations, sounds of longing, an idyllic day they had spent walking and picnicking on the Sussex downs.

He turned a sharp corner in the twisting lane and there, as brilliantly delineated in the moon's lurid glare as by a spotlight, was the lithe man in the black windcheater who had helped Margolis. The man called Ted waited, smiling and confident, poised on his toes, doubling up his left fist and showing it to Neville like a present.

Neville exclaimed: 'So! I needed you and you came!' springing at the figure before him and lashing out in a fury that unleashed all of his pent-up emotion. At that moment he did not care what the outcome of such action would be. The force of his spring took him and his opponent over in a kind of ball, cannoning into the gorse-bushes. When they jumped up a desperate fight began. They were evenly matched: both roughly the same build and equally skilled. It was a furious scrimmage, in which they used all the tricks gained by hard experience, kicking, kneeing, punches to the neck and kidneys.

A fore-arm jolt to his throat felled Neville but it was as painless as all the other blows; kneeling, he grabbed his opponent's legs and, ignoring the punches that rained on the back of his head, tugged until the man was pulled off-balance, then pushed forward as if using a battering-ram. The man's head was forced deep into the bushes and blood gushed out from a long gash in his cheek.

Neville stepped back on to the narrow path, feeling light-headed and giddy. Suddenly his senseless fury dropped from him and he was loath to continue the brutal fight in which they had both seemed victims of a mutual madness. There was a dragging noise and an exultant shout behind him but he turned too late, feeling a violent blow on the neck. There in the moonlight, which made the gorse into a black impenetrable barrier and the path shine like white sand, was the blurred image of Margolis. The image of the squat body doubled and trebled as Neville took more of the chopping blows; he fell forward into a vista of distorting mirrors; with another step he was quite lost in a maze of mirrors, and then darkness and light exploded about him.

IO

Movement = pain. Light = pain. His consciousness dealt in only such elementary equations. Neville waited a moment, then lifted his head again, and this time the experiment was less painful. The third time he opened his eyes the impression about light was modified too: it was a subdued light, coming from a table-lamp with a pink shade placed on a dressing-table.

He was in a comfortable double bed in a room where a pink colour scheme had become an obsession, so that the wardrobe was a pink and gilt affair while the carpet, blankets, eiderdown and curtains were all of various shades of the same colour. Even a doll perched on the dressing-table wore a pink gauzy dress, and there were pink tissues in a plastic box. The sheets were white though, of good linen, smelling faintly of lavender.

Neville's surroundings could not be made to match up in any way with his last memory of Margolis and some kind of an explosion. The hope that flitted through his head, that perhaps Rachel had heard the commotion across the river and brought him back to the cottage, would not bear any weight: it collapsed immediately he tried to imagine her aunt having a bedroom decked out in a show-girl's idea of glamour with two large Dutch dolls lolling in a pink wicker chair.

Stronger than the scent of lavender was the robust smell of breakfast being cooked: coffee, bacon and toast. It reminded him that he was very hungry, and he hoped to have something to eat unless he was incarcerated in Margolis's kinky establishment.

Lifting the bedclothes, he saw that he was wearing only

pants. There were two large pieces of elastoplast on his chest and another on his left knee, but there was no sign of blood or grime from the mad struggle in the gorse. He appeared to have been bathed before being tucked up so carefully. The sheets had been turned back with mathematical precision.

A glint of blonde hair at the door and a shadowy face peered round it cautiously. A tall girl, regarding him as apprehensively as Rachel had done, stepped into the room. It was hard to believe his eyes, difficult to be sure he was not dreaming. Susan Latymer said: 'Hello, Ralph! In a way I'm responsible for most of this trouble I'm afraid. I was Duff's girl . . .'

The simple concluding statement was the key to many things that had puzzled Neville, but he left her to decide when to turn it. She paused before saying anything else, coming up close to the bed and putting her cool hand on his forehead. 'You took a hard crack on the back of your head. It cut the skin and knocked you out. Then you slept. Exhausted I should think. But there's no serious damage. I told you I used to be a nurse.'

She sat down on the edge of the bed but left her hand where it was as if she was soothing a child: 'I've got a lot of apologizing to do. The subterfuge and so on. There were reasons but it's all rather complicated and will take me some time to explain . . .'

'Where am I? How did I get here? That's what is puzzling me most at the moment.'

'A flat in Flood Street, Chelsea. Belongs to an actress friend of mine who's working in Paris for the summer. I'm renting it from her. I brought you here.'

'But how? And when? I'm still puzzled. You see, the last thing I remember was being involved in a fight in Suffolk and some kind of explosion there.'

'Ah yes, the explosion. That was me too.' Susan got up from the bed and walked across to a pink chest of drawers, picking up something and then swinging round in a mock dramatic way to show it to Neville. A small automatic lay in her hand, looking like a toy. 'Duff gave it to me but I never expected to fire it. I did last night. Twice. Those men rushed off! They didn't know who was shooting, or the fact that I closed my eyes tight when I pulled the trigger. I never realized what a bang it would make.'

'But how did you come to be there? It doesn't make sense.'

'I know. Of course. I'll explain.' She smiled sympathetically, coming back to sit on the bed. 'You see, I was following you all day, right from the moment you left Eugene Morant. I was there at Burnham. I knew a way of getting quite close to Wick Farm by taking the minor road to the north and then cutting through some lanes. Eugene advised you to stick to the path by the river as it's so easy to get lost the other way. But the two men took the same route that I did – so it's fairly obvious that they were following instructions from someone who knew the area well. They had their car parked in a field quite close to where you came across the fat man. I saw you fighting with him. After you had run off the men went back to Burnham in the car, and they picked up your trail again there. So I followed behind them. There was quite a procession in fact: your red Alfa, their black Austin, my battered Mini. We all came to a halt when you had that puncture. I suppose the fact that you took your nap on the verge in the sight of passing cars stopped them tackling you then . . . ' She broke off, remembering something, touching her mouth with her fingers in a rather childish and appealing gesture. 'Oh yes, I should have said earlier that I brought you back here in *your* car, not mine. So don't worry about that. My Mini is practically a write-off, and standing in a field in Suffolk for a few days won't do it much harm . . . '

'Those two men are connected with Duff's affairs? You see, today – last night rather – wasn't the first time I met up with the fat one. He came close to drowning me in the Turkish Baths, the night you ran out on me.'

'Yes, I knew about that. I phoned the Priests on the following day to thank them for the evening, and they told me about it then. That's one reason I followed you yesterday. But those two men aren't directly involved in Duff's business. I don't want you to think he set up a situation where that kind of thing would happen to you. I have an explanation but you might not like it. You'll think I'm prejudiced.'

She seemed very reluctant to put forward her explanation. For a moment her faltering voice faded away in Neville's ears and he was left viewing one absolute fact in his life that he knew nothing would change. From that day forward he was going to have to manage his existence without Rachel. The situation was like an exposed nerve. He would be glad to be involved in anything that would take his mind off the prospect before him. He said: 'You tell me your theory and I'll tell you if I think you're prejudiced. Is that fair?'

'All right. You know by now that Duff left three letters with his bank to be forwarded: one to Eugene Morant, one to you, and one to Jack Loring. The thing is that as soon as Eugene got his he shot round to see Karin, to discuss it with her, thinking she would now be one of the partners involved in the business. She, of course, let him talk his head off without giving away the fact that she was completely in the dark. Then I think that she and that dodgy lawyer figure Woodhouse thought up a scheme whereby they'd substitute someone else to do the collecting, after having you put out of the way.'

'You think she's capable of that? I mean, ruthless enough?'

'She has . . . how shall I say it?' Susan paused reflectively. 'All sorts of capabilities. She's very astute. Very keen on the things that money can buy. Very hard too. And that's not just my opinion. Yes, I think she's ruthless enough – not to have you killed of course – I think the fat man's orders were only to put you out of action temporarily. But Duff once said to me that if you employ a thug you automatically take a risk because you're hiring muscle not brains. Having the plan outlined by Eugene must have been too much of a temptation for her. Then again, she would have been very bitter at being left out. That's my fault in a way of course. But Duff wanted to be sure I should get some of the money. I promised him that I would send Karin a share.'

'Well, what happens now? I'll press on if you want me to, but I should like to have Margolis – that's the fat man's name – put somewhere safe first. A Detective-sergeant Rossiter interviewed me after the first attack and I'd like to give Margolis's name to him, but it's a bit tricky.'

'I don't see why. I can do that. If I gave him the name and the number of their car – I followed that Austin so long the registration number's engraved on my brain – that might start Rossiter on Margolis's trail. I'll just give him the vital facts and then ring off. Anyway Margolis won't follow you any more. Only I know your next destination and *I* can check that Margolis is not behind you.' Susan seemed very keen on this idea. Her long green eyes shone with excitement as though a treat lay ahead for them and she could hardly wait.

'Okay, try that if you will. Three encounters with Margolis will last me a lifetime. But what do I have to do?'

'I can do some of it.' Susan thoughtfully steepled her fingers, then got up to pace up and down restlessly as she outlined her plan. 'First thing is – I prescribe a whole day in bed for you. Meals on a tray. Breakfast is nearly ready by the way. While you're having a rest today I'll take the document that Morant and Loring signed. Once I've signed it too, presenting it at the Midas Security Company place in the Minories will enable me to withdraw a brief-case that they hold in their vaults. I'll also collect some clothes for you from your flat. The jacket you were wearing in Suffolk was badly torn and the trousers will need cleaning too. You've got your passport and I'll get the air tickets. Tomorrow we'll be up and away. It can all be wrapped up within thirty-six hours from now . . .'

'Passport? Air tickets? May I ask where we shall be going?'

'Sorry. I keep forgetting what you know and what you don't. We shall have to go to Innsbruck. The contract that Duff had finagled was with some Austrians: the principal figure we have to deal with is a Herr Alphons Zwanzleiter.'

'Is that the man in the photograph which was enclosed in Duff's letter?'

Susan nodded and went over to pick up some papers from the pink-painted chest-of-drawers. 'Yes, that's him. "Mr A to Z" Duff called him. "Mr A to Z the financial wizard", "Mr A to Z the ace up my sleeve".'

'What else can you tell me about Mr A to Z?'

'Not much I'm afraid. Due to the way Duff planned things. Let me explain some more. It was last year when Duff decided to wrap up the contract in 1970. His various businesses weren't going too well, and he and Morant and Loring mutually decided that they would like to trade in the contract for a lump sum. Then Duff had this angina trouble and he became worried about what would happen if . . . So he worked out this plan. He said that you were someone who could be relied on in a tricky situation.' Susan broke off to touch Neville's shoulder affectionately. 'You see, I heard that story about Vierzon from Duff too. But you modestly omitted the fact that you went for the German bare-handed . . . '

Neville shrugged. 'There was no alternative. It seemed to be a simple choice of being shot sitting down or being shot going for him.'

'Your choice made a big impression on Duff nevertheless. He said these Austrian financiers were a tough and tricky lot, had to be handled by someone they couldn't bamboozle or frighten. Jack Loring was out of the running, and Duff didn't trust Eugene to handle it. Then he said, "I think I know someone who might do it for me. Someone who always bounced back". You do bounce back, don't you?'

'I used to. After three encounters with Margolis I think some of the sorbo-like quality has perished.'

'Duff laid down a plan to the last detail. I departed from it by wangling an introduction through the Priests, as I wanted to see if you were still the man Duff remembered. Then Eugene changed the plan too by consulting Karin. I'm not going to change it again. Once you are in Austria you'll know everything, and it will be just up to you how it is handled from that point. Will you go along with the plan till then – trust me – and Duff?'

The clutch of the deadhand, in the form of Duff's arbitrary request, was rigid and unchanging. If someone asked a favour in the normal way, any reservations that one had could be discussed, a limit to allegiance defined. But Duff's letter was like a directive in a will; it had to be either accepted or rejected.

Neville sat up and asked: 'May I have another look at Mr A to Z?' When Susan handed him the photograph he turned it over and pointed to the faded writing on the back. 'I checked up on that passage in Job. It's something about "He knoweth the way I take: follow me and I shall come forth as gold".'

Susan smiled. 'Yes. I phoned Eugene earlier this morning and he told me that you were concerned in case the job involved smuggling gold. I promise you that the only smuggling Duff ever did was to bring back money into this country. Something to do with the International Monetary Regulations makes it tricky. But Duff's plan takes care of that too – *you* won't have to do any smuggling! All you have to do is negotiate the sale of the documents in the brief-case, but not to Herr Zwanzleiter. He's a great industrialist and banking figure – he has a lawyer, Josef Kogler, who will handle this transaction for him. What do you say? Will you go through with it?'

'All right, I'll try it.' Neville looked directly into Susan's green eyes. 'I'm in your hands, walking ahead like a blind man.' There was more behind this sentence than Susan could be expected to understand. After discovering that the word 'perfidious' which had hovered in his mind was the right description for Rachel, he wanted to trust Susan: he found some perverse kind of pleasure in his precarious position. 'One other thing I want to ask you. How did Duff come to pick his partners? I find it very strange that he should have partners at all. When I knew him he was very much of a loner, liking to depend on himself.'

'I know. It was just the way things worked out. Duff met up with Eugene and Jack Loring in the Army, after the war was over. In the Tyrol – the Italian part I believe. Then they worked out this cunning scheme with Zwanzleiter, and they've been drawing equal shares in the business ever since.'

'In the Army? Then that's why Monica Loring was puzzled when I said that I had known Duff in the Army. I expect she couldn't understand how it was that her husband did not know me.'

'That would be it. Look, I must pop into the kitchen and see that our breakfast isn't ruined. By the way, I must lend you some dark glasses tomorrow. We want Kogler to be impressed that you're a determined, tough chap but we don't want to frighten him.' Susan handed Neville a hand-mirror. The face in the mirror looked a bit battered but most of the damage was around his eyes: his left eye was black and there was a scrape on the cheek just below it; a scratch ran parallel with his right eye-brow. What Neville did not like about the face was the fixed grin of suppressed bitterness – he felt he was going to have trouble getting rid of that expression of disillusion.

II

'*Bäuerliche gerstlsuppe* – barley soup with smoked pork,' the waiter suggested. As Neville did not rise to this idea, the waiter went on, '*Tiroler Rauchplatte . . .* ', pausing doubtfully before translating the second dish: 'Cold smoked meats with strong sauce. Very good but very hot sauce – horseradish.'

Neville sat at a prominently placed table outside the Café Hofer in the Bozner Platz at the centre of Innsbruck. It was lunch time, and he thought he ought to order some food to justify his taking a table but he did not know how long he would be there, and he was not hungry. He shook his head again.

'*Esterhazy Rostbraten mit Serviettenknödel.*' The waiter's eyes danced about as though mere words could not do justice to this dish. 'Very good sirloin steak with mixed vegetables and sour cream. Also dumplings but the dumplings special, made from breadcrumbs not flour, with chopped onions and small bits ham.'

'No, *danke.* Just some smoked ham and some *Rotwein, bitte.*' The meagre order and the fudged-up language did not disconcert the friendly waiter, who fussed around the table making minute adjustments. 'All the shops here shut Saturday afternoons,' he volunteered. 'Golden Roof – you have seen that? Built by the Emperor Maximilian with about three thousand five hundred gold-plated tiles. And the Imperial Palace?'

'Thanks, yes, I might see that.' Neville wanted to cut short the sight-seeing possibilities and pretended to stare across at the Museum Ferdinandeum as though trying to memorize each architectural detail, but his mind was busy with private bitter thoughts about Rachel. He should have been concentrating on the mysterious contents of the locked brief-case which Susan had left in his possession, and he was watching it from the corner of his eye, but his mind would not leave alone the memory of his last rendezvous with Rachel as the tongue seeks out a sore place in the mouth.

The aftermath to his aborted visit to Southwold and Walberswick was a faint feeling of biliousness, so that each of the three tasty meals that Susan had prepared had not come up to the tempting smells. Now he looked with a jaundiced eye at both rich dishes of food and tourists hurrying by with their '*Tiroler Spezialitäten*', the plastic Nativity figures, enormous candles, carved wooden pipes and gnomes. He could not conceive why anyone should want such things, but knew that the shoppers who were pleased with their purchases were all better placed than he was: over the years he had refined his interests, like whittling away at a stick, till there was hardly anything left. Losing Rachel was a deprivation he could not afford, though he would have danced round a bonfire made of all his material possessions.

Under a veneer of politeness he was in a mean, awkward mood, one which he had been barely able to hide from Susan on the flight from London. She had been a charming companion, intelligent and relaxed but showing a growing excitement as they got closer to their destination. When the plane had descended through the clouds and they first spied Innsbruck, circled by mountains, she had gripped his arm and pulled a funny face, as excited as though they had been flying to Shangri-La. He had been puzzled by this as it seemed out of character for her to be so thrilled by the prospect of laying hands on some money.

His thoughts teasingly threatened to return again to Rachel, but this was stopped by a small boy who came and stood at his table, not saying anything but looking as if he was organizing sentences somewhere behind a smooth, untroubled brow.

'*Verzeihung, sind Sie Herr Neville? Warten Sie auf eine Nachricht?* A lady asked me to give you this . . . Young lady. Message.'

Neville stood up hurriedly. 'The young lady. Where is she? Where?'

The boy pointed down *Meraner Strasse*: '*Südtiroler Platz*. Near *Hauptbahnhof*.' Neville said: 'I see. *Danke*,' puzzled at the complexity of Duff's plan which necessitated a messenger to be sent perhaps one hundred yards. Why hadn't Susan made that little trip herself? The boy handed over a coloured brochure titled WANDERKARTE INNSBRUCK/IGLS, a cornflower and a manilla envelope addressed to Neville in green ink. Neville thanked the boy again and gave him twenty *Schillings*. There was a small bulge in the envelope and it seemed probable that this would be a key for the brief-case. Neville stood up and indicated to the waiter in dumb show that he wanted to change his table for one inside the restaurant.

Going towards the back of the faintly gloomy dining-room he removed his dark glasses, catching a moody glance from a tarnished mirror. Aggressive, tensely alert, he felt just right to deal with Josef Kogler, Alphons Zwanzleiter and Margolis too, if it came to that. The ham appeared as he sat down and the waiter produced the wine with a flourish, saying '*Kalterersee – Auslese* '63'.

Neville sipped some wine before opening the envelope. The green Chancery script was in character for Susan, like her immaculate appearance: it had a cool, artistic yet unemotional look.

Dear Ralph,

Kogler will be waiting for you in the grounds of the Schloss Ambras. This is just outside Innsbruck so you will have to take a taxi. Finish your meal first and let him sweat a little. He will be wearing a cornflower in his lapel. It looks as if the deal will be easier than we had thought. The name of the game is MONEY and the price for the brief-case is £50,000 as it is the best quality hide. Zwanzleiter and Co. can easily afford such a sum. Under the contract they have been paying £10,000 a year so it's worth their while to settle now. Hold on tight to the contents of the case till you've checked the cash and then tread carefully as the time between bidding adieu to Kogler and meeting me will be the tricky bit – they might try to take the money back!

You will find a halt for a funny little tram/train at Ambras, rather tucked away in the trees. Take the tram to Igls and then take the cable-car to Patscherkofel. When you get out at 1944 metres you will see a path going round the mountain to the right. Shall be waiting for you there, holding my breath. Exciting! I feel about 105% alive! Till we meet.

Yours

Susan

It was plain to Neville that a good deal of Duff's attitude to life had rubbed off on Susan. The joking sentence about 'The name of the game . . . ' was just like one of Duff's taunting responses when things got difficult. He could see that to someone like Susan, with a highly respectable and conventional background, meeting Duff must have been like catching a glimpse of a different world, in which the rules were thrown away, all bets were open and chances were taken blindfold. And she was certainly acting with his style, proposing a meeting on the mountain. Were they going to take off from Igls by helicopter? He finished his glass of wine and opened the brochure to find a kind of picture map. The Castle Ambras lay just outside the city, and the tram-way meandered further south up wooded slopes to Igls. Susan had painstakingly added a dotted green line to show the exact route he must take from the castle to the tram-stop, and dotted the track that the tram took after it left the woods and went past two small lakes. The dots continued from the end of the tram-line to the '*Talstation*' where the cable-car started, and then again from the '*Schutzhaus*' at 1944 metres to a path marked '*Rundweg zum Patscherkofel-Gipfel*'. It was at this height that the forest covering the lower slopes of the mountain petered out: above the path the summit looked bare of vegetation, with a ski-lift going right to the top where there appeared to be some kind of radar or wireless station.

Neville committed this route to memory, then folded up the '*Wanderkarte*' and placed it firmly in his inside jacket pocket with Duff Gordon's letter.

At first sight the contents of the brief-case looked as if they would be over-priced at 50,000 farthings. A large envelope contained some photographs, there was a pocket diary and a brown-covered exercise-book. Neville opened the exercise-book and experienced a guilty shock as if he had been caught stealing something. The first page was headed in the same faded writing that he had seen on Zwanzleiter's photograph: 'Dossier on Martin Borman & ODESSA (*Organisation der ehemaligen SS-Angehörigen* – the organization of former SS members who operated escape routes over the Alps). Compiled by Eugene R. Morant, Captain, Intelligence Corps. 1945'. Underneath Morant's heading two sentences had been added in a different handwriting, in red ink: 'On October 1, 1946, Bormann was sentenced, in absentia, to death by hanging' and 'Never hang a man you do not hold – Old Nuremberg adage'.

Neville's face had become hot and flushed: it was so long since he had experienced this kind of anguish of selfconsciousness that he had forgotten what the sensation was like. He looked up from reading the exercise-book, half expecting that the other people in the restaurant might have divined his guilty secret and be staring in his direction, but they were all deep in conversation or busy devouring Tyrolean delicacies.

There were some thirty pages covered in Morant's neat hand, beginning with an outline of Bormann's career in the Nazi party. Neville skimmed through this quickly, his eye being taken by key phrases: . . . Martin Bormann, Head of the Nazi Party Chancellery . . . Bormann, the 'Brown Eminence' behind the Führer's throne . . . April 12, 1943: Bormann officially appointed *Sekretär des Führers* . . . When Bormann's house in Berchtesgaden was destroyed on April 25, 1945 his wife and children were sent to the Austrian Tyrol: Frau Bormann was discovered in May 1945 in a villa at Wolkenstein in the Grodnertal region of the Austrian Tyrol bordering on the Italian city of Bolzano . . . Bormann rumoured to have collected a hidden box of gold coins (worth about $5,000,000) originally intended for the Führermuseum in Linz and contacted ODESSA . . . American agents discovered Bormann's personal assistant, SS Colonel Wilhelm Zänder, in Aidenbach, a small village near Passau on the Austrian frontier . . . '

The last paragraph of the dossier began interestingly enough, but saved its dramatic punch till the last portentous sentence: 'Bormann's escape route on May 1 1945 from "The Citadel" (code name for the government quarter in Berlin) – through tunnel to the subway station opposite the Chancellery, then along the railway tracks to the *Friedrichstrasse* station, then to the Lehrter station near the *Ausstellungs-Park* . . . On May 25 1945, in the presence of CSM Gordon and Sgt Loring, I interviewed Franz Haller who claimed he had photographed Martin Bormann with Alphons Zwanzleiter in Patsch, near Innsbruck, on May 10th: this was later confirmed by Zwanzleiter.'

At first sight there appeared to be three negatives and nine photographs in the envelope, but these turned out to be three prints from each negative: one of them showed two men in overcoats standing near a wall of a house covered with a religious painting; the other two showed the same men photographed in a doorway. The back of each print bore an inscription in German and was signed 'Franz Haller'. The diary was in Haller's hand, with his signature, dated 1945. A single sheet of note-paper, neatly folded in half, was loosely inserted in the diary. This was a complicated statement in German, defying Neville's elementary knowledge of the language, signed 'Alphons Zwanzleiter'.

Neville's reactions to the revelations obtained by opening the case were so mixed that he would have found it difficult to disentangle any apart from surprise, but he did experience a very strong impulse to take the bag and throw it into the river that he knew flowed round Innsbruck. Admittedly he had moved into this affair rather like a sleep-walker since his mind was so taken up with Rachel, but he had not expected to be consistently tricked by Duff's friends.

When he had demurred at the idea of being involved in smuggling, Susan had urged him on with the nonsense that the 'contract' involved only some financial chicanery, instead of which he found himself taking the principal part in collecting blackmail. What a bare-faced liar Susan was – he was puzzled that she would have the nerve to face him after this had been so unequivocally demonstrated. He could not imagine how she would defend herself against the accusation which he was going to word so that it hurt before he flung her the money.

Ahead lay a menacing road and he wanted to escape from an intolerable situation, but this was the way in which Duff had wished him to repay the debt and Neville knew that he would try to do it. What stung so much was the fact that Susan had doubted whether he would go through with it, knowing the real situation, and had decided to trick him along to the point where he might feel that he was committed. He pushed away the plate of smoked ham and examined one of the photographs closely. It was an enlarged version of the doorway shot, showing only the heads and shoulders of the two men. The man with Zwanzleiter, who was supposedly Bormann, was stocky and bull-necked with dark receding hair. He had a large mole on his left temple and a noticeable scar over his right eyebrow, otherwise it was an undistinguished face, like that of his companion.

Neville replaced the contents of the brief-case, left some money to cover his bill and walked out of the Café Hofer, finding a taxi on the corner of Bozner Platz.

Seated in the rather luxurious Mercedes cab, speeding in the direction from which Susan had sent the young messenger, Neville took out the '*Wanderkarte*' and studied it again. Patsch, where the photographs of Zwanzleiter and Bormann were said to have been taken by Franz Haller, was a village like Igls at the foot of the Patscherkofel mountain, two or three miles nearer to the Brenner pass. He could see how the idea of making members of the ODESSA organization pay a special pension to three British soldiers would have appealed to Duff Gordon, and could imagine how Duff would have enjoyed returning to this area on a yearly pilgrimage to exact payment. It would have combined so many things that Duff would find more enjoyable than a legitimate business deal.

The taxi-driver was as helpful and friendly as the waiter had been, commenting on the weather to the effect that now the shower had passed over it would be fine for the rest of the day, drawing attention to the snow which capped the Serles and Habicht mountains, occasionally glancing at Neville's face in the mirror with a slightly puzzled expression. Neville realized that he had not replaced his dark glasses, and did so as the cab pulled up outside the castle walls.

Immediately he had paid off the taxi and walked through the gates of the castle grounds, Neville saw a solitary figure which he took to be Kogler: a small man in a brown suit carrying a case, trudging automatically to and fro as though on sentry duty. Neville turned round slowly as though to take in the panoramic view that the castle's site allowed of Innsbruck, with the sun gleaming on dull green copper cupolas and pointed roofs, but actually looking to see if there was anyone waiting in the vicinity to assist Kogler. The only people in sight were some obvious tourists, mostly bedecked with cameras, gathered near the gate-house and probably waiting for a guided tour to begin.

Neville grinned to himself: at that moment, just when it was most necessary, he had one advantage which no one else could know; at last he had stopped moving forward like a somnambulist. He had implied to Susan that he trusted her and said he would go on like a blind man. Now he trusted no one, and was edgily concentrating on how to get the money and survive. He stood scrutinizing the small man as if he was a specimen under a microscope. If one was forced into the crime of blackmail, then certainly the ODESSA crowd was the best group of victims he could imagine.

Swinging the brief-case, whistling one bar from 'Nowhere Man', Neville walked up to the trudging figure. Kogler's clothes viewed more closely looked like the sharp but slightly dated gear of a stage comedian. The brown suit with its rather heavy shoulders and small lapels, the unusually high polish of the tiny shoes, the carefully dented brown hat, the brown and black display handkerchief, all communicated a verve for life that was not reflected in Kogler's sad, shrewd eyes. The dark eyes had a different message, as if the small man had been foretold the course of his existence and knew it ended in a cancer ward. A cigarette trailed from the limp fingers of his free hand.

When he took in the cornflower in Neville's jacket Kogler smiled wryly, shaking the suitcase as a way of demonstrating that they had business together.

Neville moved the briefcase slightly forward to confirm the message was understood. Kogler said: 'You know this place? Beautiful, isn't it? I'm a city man myself, from Vienna. So I enjoy a day in the country. Do you speak German?'

'Yes, beautiful. I could just about order a cup of coffee in German, that's all.'

'Shall we sit down there?' Kogler pointed to a wooden seat at the end of the path and they walked along it like two office workers taking a lunch-time break in the glorious park, with sandwiches in their cases, offering to swop one of liver-sausage for one of cheese.

When they were seated Kogler rested the suitcase beside him and Neville noted that it was on a chain attached to a hand-cuff. With a touch of bravado Neville lay the brief-case down on the seat too, demonstrating that it could be removed instantly by anyone quick enough to do it. The small man said, 'Would you mind taking off your dark glasses? A foible on my part. I dislike doing business with a man when I can't see his eyes. Do me this favour?'

Neville whisked off his glasses, putting them in his breast pocket, and threw the cornflower away. Soon, he promised himself, he would be finished with this unsavoury business and throw the money at Susan Latymer's feet. A few carefully chosen words would make quite plain what he felt about her part in the affair, and no doubt carry off some of the mental bile which now affected him with an indefinable malaise.

Kogler looked at Neville's eyes and said, 'So. You've been involved in an accident?'

Neville nodded: 'Yes, I took a tumble. But I'm not accident prone. I like to think I've got a well-developed sense of self-preservation. Are we just going to swop cases? Or is there going to be a lot of chat first?'

Kogler reacted subtly to rudeness, smiling sympathetically as if he had a fellow-feeling for a slight display of nervous tension. He said: '*Meine Auftraggeber in dieser Affäre* . . .

Sorry, it happens by habit, you understand no doubt. How you would say, my masters in this affair would want me to say a few words, I'm afraid, as well as checking the contents of the case. If the contents of both cases are satisfactory then there will be no difficulty about the transfer. But first, what is your own position regarding this transaction?'

Neville spoke very slowly as if to a child. 'My position is – that I'm doing this – because I was asked to – on behalf of my friend Mr Gordon. I owed him a debt. This discharges it. If you give me the case of money, I shall ask you to give me the chain too. The chain will be my only commission. A kind of keepsake.'

'I believe you,' Kogler replied quickly. 'But the lady who has been so busy setting up this appointment, the lady of the numerous phone calls, she would be the late Mr Gordon's mistress?'

'Yes, I expect you could describe her like that. Is that important? If the contents of the brief-case are satisfactory, why worry about the lady?'

Kogler smiled enigmatically instead of replying immediately. The smile was confined to his mobile mouth; his dark eyes remained worried and untrustful. He would be always thinking, weighing up probabilities, continually tensed for real and imagined eventualities. After a long-seeming minute he said: '*Es ist eine heikle Situation. Gerade auf der Kippe.* Sorry again. It is a matter of balancing. I mean, in a situation like this – blackmail, excuse my frankness, it is necessary – the two sides are like the opposing teams in a contest, of what you call tug-of-war.' He demonstrated this point by clenching his encumbered hand and the free one and then pulling them apart as if using chest expanders. 'This tension between the two sides keeps them both on their feet. You see what I mean?'

Neville was tiring of all this Viennese subtlety. 'You mean, once you've paid this sum you're worried that the blackmailers may have kept copies, or something like that, and continue to trouble your masters?'

'Yes, something like that. Not quite. *Lassen Sie mich mal überlegen . . . wie soll ich das sagen.* Excuse me. I mean, my bosses are concerned now about the possibility of – I believe you have the phrase "rogue elephant". Someone set free and wild that they could no longer control.'

Neville was amused at the idea of Eugene Morant or Jack Loring being considered a rogue elephant. 'In my honest opinion there's not a chance in a thousand of that. This is 1970 remember. Both of the men concerned are now past that kind of thing. They'll take the cash gratefully and keep very quiet. They'd be in trouble too, if it ever leaked out, remember! And I personally don't like anything to do with this business. I just want to forget it.'

'So there is no possibility of a rogue elephant?' Kogler's bloodshot eyes were watching intently as the point was raised again.

'No rogue elephant. Believe me, once they've been paid off you'll never hear from Morant and Loring again.'

'And the lady of the telephone calls?'

'Forget it. She didn't have the nerve to see the deal through without me. I'm sure it ends here.'

'All right.' There was something unsatisfactory about the way in which Kogler said this, as though he had not been convinced about the rogue elephant but was settling meantime for something less. He put out his hand for the briefcase, signifying that the preliminary talk was over. It was Neville's turn to hang back. 'Tell me just one thing in turn. What happened to the photographer Franz Haller? Why wasn't he included in on the deal?'

Kogler moved his lips to make a hard and derisive noise of dismissal which did not accord with his projected image of the world-weary adviser. He rubbed his hands together, saying: 'Dead. Finished. A long time ago. In 1945. He was . . . ' Kogler paused to clear his throat; his timing and a faint twist of his mouth made his final sentence come out as a sneer: 'He was buried in Patsch church-yard.'

Of course Franz Haller would be dead. Neville could see that this was an obvious development of the situation. An Austrian interviewed just after the end of the war by tough customers like Gordon and Loring, not sure of his rights in the matter, intimidated by the mention of 'Security', would undoubtedly have parted with the photographs and anything else they demanded. Then, without the protection of that proof of Bormann's meeting with Zwanzleiter, there would have been nothing to stop the ODESSA organization from eliminating him like a troublesome insect.

'Right. Let's swop.' Neville said this in a cold voice. He had not expected that the affair he was involved in could be revealed in an even more unpleasant light. He undid the brief-case and handed the contents to Kogler, who looked through them and checked them against a tiny note-pad, then produced two keys and unlocked the suitcase and the hand-cuff on his wrist.

Neville opened the suitcase with as much pleasure as if he had been lifting the lid on a coffin. Kogler said: 'Fifty thousand pounds in new ten-pound notes. Are you going to count them? They've been checked twice.'

Neville lifted a few of the piles and pushed them around a little. Every moment the transaction was becoming more distasteful to him and his squeamishness made the money appear like something tainted and sickening. 'I'll take your word for it.' He locked the case and fastened the hand-cuff on to his right wrist, then walked off without saying another word to Kogler.

12

The wood near the Castle Ambras was a dark and rather gloomy place to wait for the tram/train to Igls but the surroundings mirrored Neville's mood. The firs dripped continually from the shower of rain that had passed over the valley during the morning, and trailing dead lichen hung down like tattered capes. The platform was a rudimentary affair with a tiny waiting-room in which there was one other prospective traveller, a beefy-looking woman in a Tyrolean felt hat and grey tweed suit with trousers buckled at the knee over navy-blue stockings. Immediately she saw Neville she guessed his nationality and said, 'Trough-tram soon,' as if to ward off any tiresome questions.

At the end of the toy platform there was a waste-paper basket and Neville indulged himself in a ritualistic destruction of Duff Gordon's letter, shredding it up into confetti. There was a strong acrid smell of ivy. It was only five days since the smell of Rachel's verbena hand-cream had touched off memories of Vierzon but during that time he had travelled quite a way through the land of disillusionment, and his thoughts were now as bitter as the ivy's odour. Only one person in the ODESSA affair appeared free of guilt and deserving of pity – the unfortunate Franz Haller who had inadvertently signed his own death warrant by depressing a camera button.

A break in a group of larches permitted a view of the three mountains which dominated the area. Contrasted with the jagged peaks of Serles and Habicht, the summit of Patscherkofel appeared comparatively smooth and largely covered with grass. It looked possible for a helicopter to land there, and that would certainly provide a surprise retreat from the area in case of action by the ODESSA people. What was the was planned? The humbling thought struck Neville that he point of meeting nearly at the top unless something like that might not have enough money for an air-ticket back to London, and he certainly did not intend to return with Susan. He went through his pockets and found only twelve pounds in sterling and 150 Austrian *Schillings* remaining from those which Susan had given him. He was in a ludicrous position – he visualized himself throwing the suitcase dramatically at her feet and then having to ask for his fare. In the distance, above the reiterated calling of a woodpecker, he heard an engine making slow progress up the hill. He opened the suitcase and removed two of the ten-pound notes.

The stocky-looking woman emerged from the waiting-room to exchange a smile and said that there were other small stations down the line and the 'trough-tram' might be full by the time it reached Ambras. But when the single coach arrived it was practically empty, with a handful of gossiping housewives grouped right at the front and a single male passenger at the back deep in conversation with a tiny girl. The tall man wore an old-fashioned cream linen suit and a panama hat – he had dark blue glasses and a stick. The train was a delightfully eccentric odd-looking vehicle with open platforms at both ends. The lady in Tyrolean attire joined the others at the front and Neville went further towards the back.

Immediately after leaving the Ambras halt the train entered a narrow steep gorge and made very slow progress at such an expense of effort that it seemed likely to come to a dead-stop. The tiny girl ran past Neville brandishing some stamps in her hand; the stamps she held were British ones bearing the design of the Concorde. This sight induced a strange warning feeling in Neville, and he turned round in his seat to confront the tall slightly stooping figure of 'Jamie' Woodhouse holding a heavy black automatic. Woodhouse continued to walk forward, experiencing some difficulty in doing so because of the acute angle at which the labouring train was moving. He moved the gun in Neville's direction and said, 'I'll take that case.'

Neville let go of the case and lifted his hand to display the chain. What a supreme touch of irony to be threatened by this short-sighted fool whose hands were visibly trembling. It was obvious that Margolis must have returned after the warning shots fired by Susan and managed to follow the red Alfa back to Flood Street. Now, no doubt at Karin Gordon's orders, and by dint of much nervous-making activity, myopic 'Jamie' was temporarily transformed into a desperate character. In matters of action Neville had the arrogance of experience: he knew that all plans were liable to go wrong and that the ability to improvise then enabled one to survive. He muttered, 'Fool!' in a way which made it difficult to know whether he referred to himself or the man with the Luger, then followed this with a more helpful sentence: 'Go back to the platform and I'll undo the chain there.' The suggestion appeared to take the control of the situation out of Woodhouse's hands to an extent, but he obeyed by edging backwards.

By the time they had reached the platform the situation had become rather farcical: the steep angle at which they were travelling made it extremely difficult just to stand up without performing any other action. Neville pretended to have difficulty with the key while he sorted through ways of dealing with this unhappy desperado. Simply throwing both keys away would face the would-be hijacker with the impossible situation of trying to take a bag chained to a man, but Neville wanted to keep the keys for his show-down with Susan Latymer. He undid the lock on the handcuff and moved the case forward with his left hand until Woodhouse also grasped it, then pulled it back sharply, at the same time punching Woodhouse on the point of the jaw. It was an accurate but not violent blow. Caught off balance Woodhouse fell backwards, striking his head against a steel stanchion. Neville wrested the gun from Woodhouse's feeble grasp, then twisted him round, half pushing and half booting him off the platform. His last view of Woodhouse was of brown shoes hooked over a dwarf rhododendron bush.

Neville waited till the surrealistic image of the *Alpen Rosen* with shoe blooms had vanished, then unloaded the Luger and threw it into some dense undergrowth. He had anticipated an uproar from the other occupants of the carriage but they appeared not to have noticed anything and all the Tyrolean hats were still bunched together. For a few minutes he watched the blonde pigtails of the little girl with some anxiety in case she should decide to visit the kind Englishman again for more stamps, but once the train had finished its tortuous ascent and began to speed past a golf course he stopped worrying. If it was noticed that the tall man had left the vehicle between stops there was nothing to connect Neville with such an act of folly.

On each side of the track holiday-makers were to be seen enjoying a fine afternoon in the Austrian Tyrol. Neville watched groups of people boating and bathing in the Muhlsee lake with a strange air of detachment, feeling like a visitor from another planet set down on earth for a brief visit. He had became so involved in the complicated affair bequeathed to him by Duff Gordon that now he found it hard to believe in reasonable, pleasurable, activities on a summer afternoon. He pulled out Susan Latymer's note, smoothed out the creases, and read every word again. Why did he intuitively feel that there was something odd about it, as he felt that he had detected a false note in Duff Gordon's posthumous letter? The phrase 'I feel about 105% alive' struck him as a minor verbal felicity, and he had experienced that kind of sensation himself in crossing the Bailey bridge that led to the Squireshill Marshes, but it seemed inappropriate for a girl like Susan to use in a situation involving the collection of blackmail. If she was so obsessed by money that an unpleasant way of making some really thrilled her, then all his experience in judging character had failed him. Once more he tried to visualize the confrontation on the mountain path but his imagination rebelled after the pedestrian job of setting the scene.

When the 'trough-tram' reached the end of the line in Igls Neville hurried off, expecting every minute to hear some cry raised over the man who had vanished. The route to the '*Talstation*' was firmly imprinted in his mind and it took him only a few minutes to reach the ugly concrete building and purchase a ticket for the cable-car. There were seven people waiting for the next trip but none of them appeared to be likely candidates for membership of ODESSA: a classic French family with a bored father and a petulant son, a young Austrian couple burdened with camping gear, and a little old lady. Neville, feeling nervous, went into a small bar for a glass of *Schnapps.*

Catching sight of the young Austrian couple fooling about, during which the boy demonstrated his strength by lifting the girl up to shoulder height, made Neville think enviously of the camping holiday that lay before them. How wonderful to be young and in love and setting off to walk in the mountains. He could think of nothing more desirable. His five years' service in the Army, the fact that Helen had continued to work at the hospital until she was pregnant and other factors had combined to stop them having a similarly carefree youthful period. No doubt his liaison with Rachel was a belated attempt to compensate for that.

The little old lady opened the glass door of the bar and said in a Morningside accent, 'I think you should know – the cable-car is approaching just now.' Neville thanked her and downed the rest of the *Schnapps,* wishing he had time for two or three more to give him some Dutch courage. Now that he was really close to seeing Susan again he admitted to himself that he was dreading it – his mental threats about what he would say to her were so much bluff – in the event he would probably just drop the case and turn on his heel.

The old lady from Edinburgh seemed rather nervous of the cable-car and anxious for conversation. She told Neville that she knew the area well, drew out the fact that he had never been to the Tyrol before, and recommended the water-ices at the inn *Grünwalderhof* and the chocolate cake at 'a very old *Gasthaus* at Heiligwasser where there is a pilgrims' chapel'. She asked if Neville would be going on the chair-lift to the peak, glancing rather doubtfully at his suitcase. He agreed mentally with her implication that he would look foolish suspended in the sky cradling the case, said 'no' and explained that he was only taking the cable-car ride to fill an hour before going to Innsbruck.

'Oh, what a pity! It's at the very top that you get the superb views – the glaciers of the Stubai Valley, the *Tux* Alps, the *Zugspitze* and *Kaiser* mountains . . . '

Neville was grateful that she wanted to talk, making a quick transition from a short travelogue to an account of the alpine flowers she had found, as it diverted him from thoughts of what lay ahead.

The cable-car's steady progress was turning the valley roads into chalky squiggles and the lakes to greenish-blue ink blots. The old lady always looked upwards at the blue sky framing the peak but Neville enjoyed the vertiginous aspect below as the tops of firs were whisked away. He was sorry when the machine slowed down and was brought to rest.

When the little group of travellers emerged from the concrete structure at the end of the cable-line, the French family and the Scottish lady waved and walked off towards the chair-lift. The Austrian hikers hitched up their rucksacks and departed with their arms round each other on a path going in the opposite direction to the one Susan had indicated. Neville stood still for a few moments, playing his part of the eccentric baggage-laden sightseer. It was appreciably colder than it had been in the valley and a light-weight suit was not ideal for a mountain expedition, but when he shivered it was as much from nerves as the impact of the chilly wind.

There was a continuous sound of cow-bells and several cows were grazing on the relatively flat area that extended for about one hundred yards to a point where the slopes became much steeper. As Neville walked along the path his mind was blank: he felt tired and no longer wanted to debate the rights and wrongs of the affair, or complain about the way in which he had been tricked. He said aloud: 'What's the odds.'

His shoes were unsuitable for walking along a narrow slippery path with a slope on his right hand which was becoming steeper every moment. The rocky path and the thyme-and-grass verge felt equally treacherous. Soon he had reached a point where there was a fall to the right of a thousand feet. On his left-hand side the slope upwards was less steep, with an occasional stunted bush or outbreak of rock, but it would be difficult to climb. He came to an abrupt bend where the view of a range of mountains was magnificent, but the path's edge was bordered by a sheer drop so great that he could not estimate it.

Neville looked up from the dizzying prospect to see the back view of a man standing at an equally dangerous point on the path some fifty feet ahead. The man, dressed in a fawn windcheater and dark blue trousers, turned awkwardly, swinging one leg round stiffly. The palms of Neville's hands became wet and his heart thumped. Could this be an emissary from the ODESSA organization? He did not fancy his chances either in wrestling on the slippery path or in trying to run back along it.

He moved forward carefully, concentrating on treading each step firmly, and the other man limped towards him. Despite the cripple's gait he moved in an indolent manner, as if he was mooching down Bond Street instead of within a few inches of a precipice. Fast on the shock of the encounter for Neville came the greater one of recognition. The limping man was Duff Gordon. He was bald apart from grizzled hair at the sides, but otherwise he looked much as he had done in 1944. Gordon acknowledged Neville's shocked expression with a grin. He was wearing a blue checked shirt open at the neck and white shoes with rubber soles. Despite the limp he looked extremely fit. He held a small automatic in his right hand, and the negligent way in which he carried it seemed to emphasize its murderous capabilities.

'I'm sorry, Ralph. Very sorry about all the lies and the tricks. But I needed your help and I couldn't tell you the truth . . .'

'What is this? *Tricks?* Who was drowned? Your daughter Liz told me they had found your body.'

'Yes, Liz. I'm sorry about Liz too. But I had to vanish, Ralph. The income tax people were after me and there was a chance of doing eighteen months in one of Her Majesty's prisons . . . ' Gordon thumped his chest with his left hand. 'Eighteen months – with my ticker trouble I couldn't spare that much time. Besides, there were other reasons. Too many to go into now. So I needed to vanish. I wanted to find a big hole to crawl into. Then I came on this body when I was out sailing. A drowned body in a creek. It was like being dealt a running flush or being handed the keys to the bank. You can't understand how I felt. It was the solution. So I went out again in my boat and Susan took a hired motor-cruiser. I wrecked the yacht and dumped the body on a sandbank where I knew it would be found if there was a search. He was about my size and had false gnashers like me. And the crabs had been eating his face. So . . .'

Neville said: 'It's a rotten business. A dirty trick to play on your daughter.'

Gordon grinned wryly: 'You've never felt desperate. I can see that. Like being threatened with prison gates and suddenly seeing a way out. Try it sometime and then you can lecture me.'

'Why drag me into it?' Neville shouted this and the last words echoed mockingly.

Gordon swung his stiff leg forward. 'I did this jumping on to the motor-cruiser – broke my fucking leg. Talk about the best laid plans. I thought we'd run into tough opposition in trying to get away with the cash and I needed a strong right arm. And you did say you owed me a favour. Remember?'

'Yes. I remember. And I've paid it off too. What's the gun for?'

Gordon smiled thinly. 'They're very bad boys, the crowd we're playing with. And the game's not over yet. Quite a way to go.'

'That was another reason for you wanting to "die" wasn't it? If you were "dead" then you were no longer a threat to the ODESSA people. But what about the others, Morant and Loring? Me too, for that matter?'

Gordon shrugged. 'I don't think there will be any vendetta, sending assassins to Britain is out I reckon. This is the dangerous place – we're doing the tightrope walk now. Morant and Loring are all right.'

Neville's brain was churning over unpleasant thoughts with a final sense of disillusionment. This ruthless egotist was the man he had so admired. Suddenly he was struck by an idea that was even more unpleasant. 'The money. You don't intend to share it with them! You're going off with the lot. And I go back home as the scapegoat, with a story they'll never believe?'

Gordon said nothing but raised the gun a fraction, his bright blue eyes searching Neville's for an indication of his thoughts. Both men were silent for a hard-breathing minute, then Gordon sniffed and rubbed his nose with the back of his left hand. 'Jesus, it's freezing here. I've been waiting for an hour. Let's have the bag and I'll be off. We're quits. Surely your life was worth what's in the bag?'

Neville said: 'Is that a question or a threat? Oh to hell with you.' He tightened his grip on the bag and stepped backwards.

'Don't be stupid, Ralph. I need that money. This is my only way of getting some. Morant and Loring – they're okay. I did all the scheming through the years, every bit of it. I want the bag.' Gordon raised the gun again so that it nearly pointed at Neville but his hold on it still appeared casual, and he was grinning as though they were having an amiable argument over some unimportant matter.

'All right.' A sense of grievance in Neville snapped and he was aware only of a cold anger that would not heed any advice. 'You want the bag.' He said this in a silly voice, parroting Gordon's claim. 'Here – catch.' He swung the case forward, throwing it slightly to the right, judging the distance cruelly so that if Gordon had not been lame he might just have intercepted it. The suitcase went up and out for six feet then described a graceful parabola, falling for perhaps one thousand. Both men watched its fall with fascination. It bounced twice and came to rest on a ledge which only a mountain climber equipped with ropes could reach.

Gordon stared down as though he could not believe his eyes, moving his left arm out in some kind of hopeless restraining gesture. When he looked up again he said to Neville: 'Why, you chancy bastard!' Mixed with surprise and anger there was some kind of grudging admiration. 'You fucking fool! Now what? Are you happy now? Satisfied?' He stared down again at the case, shaking his head and putting the small automatic absently into his jacket pocket. He shook his head from side to side and appealed to an invisible audience: 'I had to pick a saint.' He grinned faintly as Neville had known him to in other moments of adversity and Neville felt a surge of affection for the ghost of the old Duff Gordon.

A shot rang out as a kind of echo to the word 'saint'. The loud, hard, unmistakable sound of a high-powered rifle, followed by an authentic booming echo. Neville threw himself forward under a projecting ledge of rock as a second shock reverberated. When he looked up he saw that Duff had fallen too and was lying spreadeagled across the path. There was a black hole in his neck and a stain on the cotton jacket that was growing larger every second – and it was a dead hand that was extended towards Neville, with the palm open, as if in a last gesture of reconciliation.

fiat

More about Penguins and Pelicans

Penguinews, which appears every month, contains details of all the new books issued by Penguins as they are published. From time to time it is supplemented by *Penguins in Print*, which is a complete list of all titles available. (There are some five thousand of these.)

A specimen copy of *Penguinews* will be sent to you free on request. For a year's issues (including the complete lists) please send 50p if you live in the British Isles, or 75p if you live elsewhere. Just write to Dept EP, Penguin Books Ltd, Harmondsworth, Middlesex, enclosing a cheque or postal order, and your name will be added to the mailing list.

In the U.S.A.: For a complete list of books available from Penguin in the United States write to Dept CS, Penguin Books Inc., 7110 Ambassador Road, Baltimore, Maryland 21207.

In Canada: For a complete list of books available from Penguin in Canada write to Penguin Books Canada Ltd, 41 Steelcase Road West, Markham, Ontario.

Watcher in the Shadows

Geoffrey Household

Charles Dennim is forced to realize that a ruthless killer is after him. Revenge for an incident in a German extermination camp is the motive: police protection offers little comfort. Coolly, Dennim decides to plant himself out in the country – a tethered goat to lure the tiger.

'Splendid stuff, as good as John Buchan's best' – *Daily Express*

Not for sale in the U.S.A. or Canada